JAN VAN MERSBERGEN

*TRANSLATED FROM THE DUTCH
BY LAURA WATKINSON*

Peirene

Morgen zijn we in Pamplona

AUTHOR

Jan van Mersbergen, born 1971, stands at the forefront of new Dutch writing. He has completed five novels. His concise and tense style has earned him critical acclaim and a wide readership. Jan has been nominated for numerous prizes, among them the BNG New Literature Prize 2007 and 2009, and the European Book Prize 2010. *Tomorrow Pamplona* was first published in Dutch in 2007 and has already been translated into German and French.

TRANSLATOR

Laura Watkinson studied languages at St Anne's College, Oxford, and now lives in Amsterdam. She translates literary fiction from Dutch, German and Italian.

MEIKE ZIERVOGEL
PEIRENE PRESS

I adore the deceptive simplicity of this story. On the surface, the fast moving plot, the short sentences, the ordinary words make the text as straightforward as punches in a boxing match. But just as physical conflict stirs deep emotions, so too does this book as it focuses on a single question: how do you choose between flight and fight?

First published in English in 2011 by
Peirene Press Limited
17 Cheverton Road
London N19 3BB
www.peirenepress.com

Originally published in Dutch as
MORGEN ZIJN WE IN PAMPLONA
Copyright © 2007 by Jan van Mersbergen and Cossee Publishers, Amsterdam

This translation © Laura Watkinson, 2011

This publication has been made possible with the financial support
from the Dutch Foundation of Literature.

Jan van Mersbergen asserts his moral right to be identified as the author of
this work in accordance with the Copyright, Designs and Patents Act 1988

Printed in Great Britain by T J International, Padstow, Cornwall

ISBN: 978-0-9562840-4-4

Designed by Sacha Davison Lunt
Typeset by Tetragon
Photographic image: Andrea Pistolesi / The Image Bank / Getty Images

JAN VAN MERSBERGEN

TRANSLATED FROM THE DUTCH
BY LAURA WATKINSON

Peirene

Tomorrow
Pamplona

1

A boxer is running through the city. He heads down a street with tall buildings on either side, darts between parked cars, runs diagonally across a junction, down a bike path, crosses a bridge and follows the curve of the tram tracks. Anyone passing would think he was in training. But he's running faster than usual. His breathing is out of control. His eyes are wide.

His boxing boots fly silently over the pavement. Fragments of sentences echo around his head, accompanied by the ringing of a bell. Disconnected words thud against his eardrums, buzzing sounds, distorted, far away. Then suddenly they become clear.

Stop.

He lands a punch.

Stop that!

He lands another punch. Again he hears a bell, sharper and louder than before. Stop, someone screams. He feels a hand on his shoulder, fends it off with a jab of his elbow. He throws a left hook, hits the man square in the face and turns back to his opponent.

Stop that! he hears again. He lands another punch, and another, and another.

He crosses a busy main road and runs into a park. He comes to a patch of grass with a bronze statue in the centre, a woman holding a child in the air as though she wants to entrust it to the clouds.

The boxer slows, panting, and looks at the statue. He sits down on a bench. The bushes and trees stand motionless between him and the street with the tramlines. Dark grey clouds slide past behind the trees. There are no birds, not even pigeons.

He feels fine drops of rain on his face. The leaves on the trees move gently in the breeze. A man in a denim jacket is standing on the other side of the park, beneath the awning of the cigar shop on the corner. He's looking in the boxer's direction. Another man comes out of the shop, lights a cigarette, and says something to the man in the denim jacket, who replies without taking his eyes off the boxer. The smoke dissolves in the air. The boxer looks down at his legs and at the wood of the bench, as it slowly darkens in the rain.

He hears footsteps. For a moment, he seems resigned to his fate. He waits for a deep voice to say something, to speak his name, to pin him to the bench. When it comes, the tone isn't what he expected: Hey, you're Danny Clare, aren't you?

The man walks over and stands in front of him, turns up the collar of his denim jacket. The other man stops behind his friend, off to one side. With no expression on his face, the boxer looks at the two men.

You are him though, aren't you? The boxer?

Danny gets up.

We saw you, says the man in the denim jacket. He tugs at his collar again, trying to shield his neck from the rain.

Against that big blond guy, it was. The Hungarian.

The other man corrects him: Bulgarian.

Danny doesn't react. He just clasps his hands.

Good fight, that was.

The cigarette falls to the wet gravel and the man crushes it with his foot. The two men smile at the boxer. The man in the denim jacket says something else, but his voice fades away and Danny looks down at the cigarette butt, which is still smouldering, and then at his feet. Now he can hear words from his conversation with Pavel, at the boxing school. And there's that click in his head again, when it all fell into place, and the click that came afterwards when everything around him imploded and went black.

I don't know what you're talking about, he says. He runs to the park exit, leaving the men and the statue behind. He goes through the gate, crosses the tramlines and races along the brick wall and around the corner. Finally, he reaches a busy dual carriageway, with an endless stream of cars flowing out of the city. That's the road he wants. The rain sweeps against his face. He runs past a supermarket and sees a black kid pushing a line of shopping trolleys inside. He passes beneath a viaduct with drops of rainwater clinging to its solid metal girders. Reflections of the posters on the walls ripple dimly in the puddles. He stops in the shelter of a tree by a big roundabout. On his right, a railway line hangs high above the street. He sees the station just beyond the roundabout. A long train is pulling in, its wheels screeching. The boxer puts his hands in his pockets. His keys, his loose change, his mobile – it's all still in the changing room at the boxing school.

The traffic spins around the roundabout and fans out along the roads leading to and from the city. He takes the road to the motorway. He crosses over, walks through the long grass in the centre of the roundabout, waits for a gap in the traffic, crosses again, stands by the roadside and raises his thumb. A car soon stops for him. There's an old man at the wheel. I can take you a few kilometres down the motorway, he says.

The boxer nods and gets in.

I'll drop you off at the petrol station. You'll be able to get another ride from there, no problem.

The man accelerates gently, navigates a few bends and heads onto the motorway. Opera plays on the radio. The voice pierces through the noise of the engine. When Danny looks at the radio, the man turns the knob and the music becomes louder. The voice grates on his nerves. They sit in silence for a few minutes. Then the man takes the exit for the petrol station. When they reach the pumps, Danny thanks him and steps out of the car into the smell of petrol.

You're welcome, says the man.

Danny slams the car door.

*

He walks over to the verge just beyond the canopy of the petrol station. The rain is coming down harder now. His hair is plastered to his forehead and his T-shirt is sticking to his chest. Cars race past, just patches of colour on the other side of the crash barrier, all heading in the direction he wants to go. Half-heartedly, without looking at the drivers, he holds up his thumb at every car that drives back onto the motorway with a full tank.

He sees a big estate car. A family car. Automatically, he raises his thumb again. When the car stops, it's a moment before he realizes he can now walk over to the open door and ask the question he needs to ask. He reaches the car and leans over, but not too far. The roof hides his eyes from the driver.

Where do you want to go? A hurried voice.

He straightens up, glances over his shoulder. The rain beats down on the roof and the windscreen wipers squeak. He shows his face to the driver and says: I'm heading that way.

He points down the motorway, just as the wind picks up and the rain starts rattling on the bonnet. The man tells him to get in, says he shouldn't be standing out there in the rain.

Beyond the canopy of the petrol station, he sees silhouettes of buildings huddled together in the distance, where the cars are coming from, where he came from. A few office blocks rise up above a serrated horizon. For a moment, he thinks about saying goodbye to that image, even though it means nothing to him. He stares at the silhouette of the city. Then he climbs into the car and shuts the door. There are scraps of paper on the floor, sweet wrappers. A plastic bottle without a top. The car moves onto the slip road, lets another car overtake and moves into the right-hand lane. Danny asks the driver if he minds his upholstery getting wet.

Not a problem. Just be glad you're inside and dry, the driver says. Danny looks at him and tries to smile. The man is blinking, a tic.

The driver's older than him. Maybe mid-forties. And he's a lot smaller, with narrow shoulders and pale, thin arms. He's wearing white trousers and a white polo shirt and Danny can see the beginnings of a paunch.

You been there long?

He doesn't know. Could have been a couple of minutes, could have been quarter of an hour. He spots a digital clock between the speedometer and some other dial with a needle. Not too long, he says. The two dots between the digits blink and he realizes that, even though the man is asking him questions, the answers don't really matter. The numbers on the clock change. He stares at them until they change again. Then his gaze falls on a frame stuck to the dashboard. There's a photo in it. A woman with long, straight hair. Two children standing in front of her, a boy and a girl. The woman's hand rests on the girl's shoulder.

He turns away, swears at the window and says her name, his breath steaming up the glass. Damn it, Ragna. It's as though she's sitting in the back seat and he's whispering to her.

The car passes beneath a flyover and for a moment the window darkens and he's looking at his reflection. He turns his head again. As the car drives back into the grey light, he stares at the bonnet, at the white line stretching ahead of the car, shakily trying to maintain its course, scratching away at his thoughts.

They overtake a lorry. Splashing circles of rainwater spray out around its huge wheels. The driver has a roll-up in his hand. He looks down at Danny. At his wet clothes, his hair. His face. They accelerate and Danny watches the lorry growing smaller in the wing mirror. When it's disappeared, he leans against the window. He shivers.

Need a towel?

I'm almost dry.

There's one in that bag behind you.

On the back seat are a few carrier bags, a sports holdall, a rucksack and a big red grocery bag lying on its side. He notices a wholemeal loaf, a packet of biscuits, a bottle of mineral water. In that green one, says the man. Danny pulls over the sports bag, unzips it and takes out a towel. He dries his hair, presses his face into the towel. It smells of fabric softener. He hangs the towel over the back of his seat and leans against it.

The driver says: Better now?

He's not very comfortable, but he nods.

Could you put your seatbelt on?

What?

Would you put your seatbelt on?

Danny pulls the belt and clicks it shut. His cold T-shirt is sticking to his body. Something is pressing into his lower back. Something hard and pointed. He doesn't move.

The motorway is wide, three lanes and a hard shoulder. They cruise along in the middle lane for a while. The driver occasionally glances over at him.

I often pick up hitchhikers.

Danny remains silent.

Not many people stop for hitchers nowadays, but I do. The driver coughs. I'm just interested. To hear what they have to say.

Danny looks at the driver, who continues: It doesn't matter whether they're in the car for a few hours or just a few minutes, they all tell me something. About their work. About home, relationships, pets. All kinds of things. Their lives, the stuff they get up to. And sometimes it's not the nicest stuff. I mean, it's not that nice to listen to.

Who says I'm going to tell you anything?

The man blinks and smiles.

*

He switched off the fluorescent lights, walked down the corridor to the changing room, sat on the bench in his usual spot and pulled a towel around his shoulders. He was still panting. He bit through the tape on his right wrist, clasped the end of the bandage between his teeth, pulled it loose and freed his other hand. The bandages spooled onto the tiled floor between his feet. He stood up, walked over to the sink, turned on the tap and drank. Then he cupped his hands, filled them with water, washed his face and splashed water onto his hair and neck.

Danny?

Richard Rosenberger's face appeared around the door. A bunch of keys dangled against his thigh. His hair was swept back.

Hey, Rich.

The others all gone home?

Yeah.

Well?

Danny nodded. Looking good. He sat back down and undid his laces.

I only saw the first fifteen minutes.

Against that black guy?

Yeah.

He's lighter.

Not much.

But then he's taller.

Yeah, a bit. My dad always said you shouldn't pay attention to that sort of thing. Height. And it's only the scales that should be paying any attention to your weight. That's what he always said.

When's your brother get back?

You missing him?

He's good to train with.

He'll be back in a week.

Neither of the men spoke for a while.

You ever seen that Bulgarian fight? Danny asked, breaking the silence.

Once, in Germany. That's where he trains. At Azzopardi's.

Danny nodded. Rich sat down on the bench opposite him, resting his elbows on his knees.

The time I saw him he was fighting a Russian. I was with my dad. One of the last fights he saw. The Russian guy had won twenty-one fights in a row – and then he came up against Hristov.

Okay, said Danny. He took off his boots and wiggled his toes.

What about tonight? The other guy no good?

He's got more power than that black guy, but he's slow. Spent too much time standing still.

Hristov's slow too.

Not that slow.

No, not that slow, Richard agreed. He stood up, ran his hands through his hair and said: Just stay cool.

That's what your dad always said.

Yeah, why do you think I took over this place?

*

There's a red van in front of them with PVC pipes on its roof. All he can see in the wing mirror is wet tarmac and a few cars. Then a flash of colour on the floor, orange and yellow, a couple of letters. An A and a G. The wet floor. A bare leg lying in a puddle in the corner. The lights above him reflected on either side of the leg like small yellow globes.

Where do you want to go?

He nods at the windscreen and says: That way.

That way?

Yes.

The driver looks over at him.

I need to know where to drop you off.

I'll get out whenever you want me to.

The man leans forward a little, blinks a few times, and says: I won't be stopping any time soon.

He steers into the left-hand lane, grips the steering wheel and accelerates. I'm just going to keep on driving for a while yet.

That tic again. Everything is still, except for his eyes.

You mean you're going to drive through the night?

Yes, if I can. The driver blinks a few more times. Then he says: I get the feeling you'd rather not say where you're going, but you're in my car, so you might at least tell me what's up.

A sign beside the motorway indicates an exit just over a kilometre away.

You can drop me off there.

They drive past the sign. The exit looms in the distance.

There?

Yes.

That's where you want to get out?

Danny rests his large hands on his thighs and hangs his head. His breath quickens. He closes his eyes and everything goes dark. For a moment, all he can feel is the hum of the car and the beating of his heart. The two rhythms slowly synchronize. The sound and direction of the car remain the same. When he opens his eyes, they're passing the sign with the white arrow and he sees the rain pelting against it. The turning and the white line curve away from them.

Hey, let me know when you really want to get out.

Thanks, he whispers.

The car's speeding up now, the blinking becomes faster too, and the boxer looks at his forearms, at the bulging veins. He stares over the top of the wing mirror. Square buildings line the motorway, huge toy blocks in the watery landscape. He sees a showroom with a gleaming new car in the window, like a trophy in a display cabinet. They stay in the right-hand lane for a long time. Now and then, the wheels brush the solid white line and the high-pitched sound that buzzes through the car reminds him that they really are moving. They're heading somewhere else.

*

The windscreen wipers swish backwards and forwards. Road signs appear within the glass rectangle as it is wiped clean over and over again. They approach Utrecht, leave it behind. A fat black fly buzzes against the window behind him. It twitches nervously along the rubber strip. They overtake a line of cars. Each of the back seats is occupied by a gaggle of young boys, about ten years old. Some of them are wearing football shirts. Yellow shirts with black stripes. There's a boy in a goalkeeper's shirt in the front car. As they go past, he pushes two big goalie gloves up against the window, waggles his head between the gloves and pokes his tongue out.

The driver rests his hands on the steering wheel. Is your T-shirt dry yet?

Yes.

There's a dry one in that big bag behind you. You can wear that if you like.

I'm almost dry.

The man reaches out to feel the sleeve of his T-shirt. You'll catch cold.

Danny shifts in his seat. Something's poking into him again. He shifts forward, reaches behind him and pulls a blue toy car from the crack of the seat.

My son's, says the driver. It's got opening doors.

It's an Alfa Romeo 1300. Danny turns it over. Through the tiny window, he can make out a plastic steering wheel and seats. The car has a tow bar and a number plate. It even has suspension. Front and rear. The blue paint's worn off in places, down to the grey of the metal beneath. He pulls open the driver's door with his fingernail. Then closes it again.

Pretty cool, eh?

Danny opens the door on the driver's side again. Then he flicks open the passenger door. I used to have an Alfa, he says.

Like that one?

No, but it was still an Alfa.

Silence. Then the driver says: My name's Robert.

The boxer looks at the man out of the corner of his eye. Robert, he echoes, closing the toy car's doors with a click.

What about you?

Daniel. But everyone calls me Danny.

Danny.

Robert takes his right hand off the steering wheel. It looks as though he's about to shake Danny's hand, but he doesn't. He puts his hand back on the wheel, leans forward and studies Danny. Then he looks back at the tarmac.

I'm in insurance.

Danny nods.

What about you? What do you do?

Danny puts the Alfa on the dashboard. The toy car rolls from one side to the other, gets stuck on a bump, goes into reverse, bounces back and hits the bump again. He says: I'm a boxer.

A boxer?

Yes.

You fight in proper matches?

He hesitates, then says: I just fought my last fight.

Are you well known?

Yes.

What's your surname?

Clare. Danny Clare.

Robert looks at him. Yeah, now that you mention it. You say you've just had your last fight?

Yes.

Well? Did you win?

He sees Ragna's face again. Her eyes are closed and her hair is spread out over the pillow. The white moonlight is shining through the roof window, illuminating one of the corners of the pillow. He looks away and takes hold of the soft fabric of his trousers, squeezing it between his thumb and index finger.

Yes, I won, he says.

Robert doesn't ask him any more questions. A bird flies low over the meadows, its shadow gliding beneath it like a dark patch on the wet grass. Danny winds down the window, rests his elbow on the door and feels the fresh wind on his face and his arm.

*

He began training at seven o'clock. At that hour, there were only a few lads at the Rosenbergers' boxing school, working with their stocky Turkish trainer. Richard said he'd once been the Turkish army welterweight champion. He'd been living in Amsterdam for ten years and he certainly wasn't a welterweight any more.

Danny stood in his usual corner, beneath the steamed-up windows. The boys worked through their programme. Every time the bell went and they took a breather, they looked over at Danny. When the bell rang for the next five minutes, they carried on training. Danny warmed up with some stretches, followed by a few strength exercises on the mat.

Then Ron arrived. He and his brother Richard were almost like two peas in a pod. The only difference was that Ron was completely bald – and he'd once been a boxer himself and had broken his nose at some point. He was bigger than Danny and must have outweighed him by twenty kilos. Danny said hello to them and when Ron had got changed into his training gear he helped Danny put on his gloves. Ron took the boxing pads out of the cupboard. The junior boxers had all gone home by then and the seniors were trickling into the room one by one. Ron set the clock and they worked through a few jabs and combinations. They trained for over seventy-five minutes. Danny held back because the other boxers were all amateurs. He gave them the occasional pointer. He sparred with a guy from Russia who'd trained at boxing schools in Tula and Kiev, and who didn't say a word, just smiled whenever Danny explained something to him. Towards the end of each interval, Ron stepped things up, clapping to set the tempo and to encourage the boxers to keep it up until the bell rang. Ron's T-shirt was damp and his bald head was beaded with sweat.

Danny went off for a shower after the training session and then headed to the canteen. One of the younger boxers was sitting there with a bowl of water in front of him. He was a tough-looking Surinamese lad with drowsy eyes and he was wearing a padded jacket with a huge hood. Ron came out from behind the bar with a plastic mouth guard in his hand. He dropped it into the warm water. His first gum shield, he said to Danny.

When's your fight?

Two weeks, said the boy.

His first match, said Ron. He squeezed the mouth guard to see if it was soft enough. Then he shook the water off it and told the boy it wasn't going to hurt.

The boy nodded. Ron told him to open his mouth and said: If it fits okay, just bite down on it.

He held the back of the boy's head with one hand, pushed his head against his hip, and pressed the mouth guard onto the boy's top row of teeth with his other hand. The boy closed his eyes and put a brave face on it.

Don't worry. You're in the hands of an expert, Danny said.

The boy just groaned.

Bite down on it for a while, make sure it fits properly.

Ron left the boy sitting there while he went to the bar. He poured himself a coffee and then took a carton of fruit juice out of the fridge for Danny and poured him a glass. Danny downed the juice in three gulps. Ron topped him up.

That long enough? the boy grunted.

You have to keep it in all night, said Ron. Oh yeah, and all the way through Christmas dinner too.

The boy laughed. He carefully removed the guard and studied the imprint of his teeth. Then he thanked Ron and left him alone with Danny.

Ron poured out a bowl of peanuts and joined Danny at the bar.

Right, mate, he said. If you fight like that, he'll be down within three rounds.

Ron stuffed a handful of peanuts into his mouth.

I heard someone else was scheduled to fight him.

That's right.

What happened? Did he drop out?

Don't know. Rich sorted it.

Danny took a swig of juice, put the glass down on the bar and looked out at the sky through the tall windows. The clouds were grey.

Do you know why Aaron's not boxing?

No idea.

When I heard there was a fight coming up with the Bulgarian guy, I thought he'd be doing it.

Don't ask me, Ron said with a shrug.

Aaron's a good boxer and he's younger than me. I thought he'd fight. Or that other guy. What's his name? The one who always wears those red shorts.

Sando?

He's in my weight class too.

You seen him recently?

No. Has he stopped coming?

I don't know.

Is he back inside again?

No, it's not that. Rich bumped into him somewhere or other not long ago. He was off to another of those salsa parties of his.

Salsa?

Haven't you heard? He goes to these salsa parties. To pick up women.

Danny looked at him.

He's never told you? said Ron. He goes along to the parties, but it's certainly not for the salsa. It's just for the birds. They all want to shag him.

What? Sando? Sando from here?

You really didn't know? They pick him up and they take him home. And they actually pay him for the pleasure.

What? They pay him for sex?

Yeah. Rich said he was all done up like a dog's dinner. Because he'd had such a good night the last time. Know how much they pay? You'll never guess. A hundred a go. He made four hundred in one night the last time. With the same woman. Then another hundred in the morning. Says he's at it like a bloody rabbit.

Bunch of madwomen, said Danny.

Rabbits, the lot of them, Ron said. He looked at Danny and grinned. Hey, I can see the cogs turning. If that tosser gets a hundred a go, reckon I could ask two hundred.

More like three.

Ron smiled and said: All I know is they wanted you to fight the Bulgarian.

Danny shifted on his barstool.

You ever done any work for him?

Who? Gerard Varon? Ron cupped his hands around his coffee. Training sessions, he said. Only after Dad was gone though. He wasn't that keen on him.

They say he takes good care of his people.

You'd have to ask my brother about that, Ron replied. He knows about that sort of thing. All I know is I've never had any problems with him. Can't say the same about Dad though. He always called Varon a dirty old man, but that's what he called everyone who wasn't wearing training gear.

Danny slid down from his stool and stood there, looking at Ron. I seem to remember seeing your dad in a suit from time to time. With a tie and everything.

Yeah? Well, that must have been when he was off to visit the queen.

*

They're driving along a concrete section of the motorway, the car thudding over the ridges between the slabs. The blue Alfa 1300 rolls from one side of the dashboard to the other. Danny picks it up, spins the wheels, tests the suspension and plays with the doors. Robert says: Did I tell you where I'm going?

No.

Spain. Pamplona. His voice is lower now. To the bull running. Ever heard of it?

Of course, Danny lies.

But you've never been to Pamplona?

No.

Then you can't possibly understand it.

A long silence. They drive past fields that are crisscrossed by straight drainage ditches. Danny sees a row of willows leaning over a ditch, their roots in the water.

He rolls the toy car across his palm. He slides over to the window and says: So you're going to Pamplona?

Yeah, for the twelfth year. It starts tomorrow morning. I'm going to run with the bulls.

Robert holds his breath and his chest swells out over his belly. He coughs. Between the blinks, Danny sees a sparkle in Robert's eyes, like a little boy who's about to do something naughty.

Tomorrow morning, I'm going to come face to face with a bunch of bulls, Robert continues. He taps the steering wheel. I'll be standing there on one of those streets in Pamplona, in my white shirt, together with all those other people in their white shirts. Then they let the bulls out and you'd better start running.

Running? Danny asks. It's hard for him to find a neutral tone, but he manages.

Robert nods. Yeah, as fast as you can and as far you can. He blinks. Down those narrow streets, in your white shirt and white trousers. With a red handkerchief around your neck. Which is also somewhere in one of those bags.

A thought flickers at the back of Danny's mind. He grips the Alfa tightly. One of the wheels pricks his skin. He says: You actually let a herd of bulls chase you?

Yes. Six massive bulls, each of them over five hundred kilos. He points at the car in front of them. See that car? One single bull is more powerful than that. So imagine six of them coming for you.

Robert waits for the cars in the left-hand lane to pass the Volkswagen. Then he overtakes too. The motorway curves uphill.

Danny pulls at the seatbelt and lets it spring back into place.

So why exactly are you going there?

What?

Why are you going all the way to Pamplona to let a bunch of bulls chase you?

Yeah, I know. You're probably thinking: What the hell's he doing? A man like him, driving all the way through France and down to Spain, just for that. You wouldn't be the first to wonder. Plenty of people think I've got a screw loose. But I still go. Every single year.

He looks in his wing mirror and overtakes a lorry, an old Scania with a long bonnet. He chuckles to himself.

So do you do it for the kick?

Danny puts his hand on the window winder.

Try to imagine, Robert says, what it feels like when they release the bulls. The noise is incredible. Your whole body's shaking. It's like your heart's racing but standing still at the same time. And then, when the people around you start moving and you know the bulls are coming, it just gets worse and worse. You hear the bulls coming closer. You feel the ground shaking beneath your feet. And when you see that first bull and it's time to run, everyone starts screaming. You can't even think. All you can do is run as fast as your legs will carry you.

Robert tilts his head back and stares up at the roof of the car. Then he glances over at Danny, gives him an awkward wink and looks back at the road.

Danny clenches his teeth and looks in the wing mirror, at the grey clouds. A thin strip of blue sky is appearing at the top of the windscreen.

They've been doing it for over four hundred years. Can you think of anything we've been doing for that long in the Netherlands? Except maybe for boxing.

The two men look at each other for a moment.

It's a tradition, Robert continues. It's a celebration. It's danger. It's real life.

But why would you want to do something like that?

Why would I want to do something like that? Robert laughs. He pauses before continuing: I have a family and a house and a nine-to-five job, he says. Five days a week, all year round. Except for that one week in Pamplona.

So Pamplona's your escape?

It's more than an escape, Robert replies. And it's not just about the kick. You've got to have your own reason for running with the bulls. I once spoke to this man in Pamplona, a Spanish guy, who said he went every year. He was wearing this long white robe thing, so I asked him why he was going around in a dress. It wasn't a dress, he said. It was a penitential robe. And Pamplona was his pilgrimage. He went there to wash away his sins.

And is that what it is for you? A pilgrimage?

Robert hesitates. I don't know, but there's something true in what he said. I work all year for my family, but half the time I don't even know why I'm doing it. You get what I'm saying? Let's just say I'm not the easiest of people. Bit of a naughty boy sometimes, if you know what I mean. And, somehow, Pamplona helps. When you're standing there and those bulls are coming for you, you forget everything else. You don't even need to be wearing a dress.

You could just join a monastery.

But these Spanish guys, their religion is on the streets. At least that's the way it was for that one man I met. He doesn't need to crawl through Spain on his knees the way people used to. He just goes to the fiesta once a year. It's like an express pilgrimage: three minutes of running have the same result as months of crawling. You get it?

Robert's driving faster now. The car's flying down the motorway. Danny sees the meadows whizzing by and the trees flicking past and realizes that he really has left it all behind. The car is pushing ahead and, all around him, everything is rolling and moving. He swears to himself. Crawling, he thinks, down on your knees.

And that's what it's all about, says Robert. But you have to experience it for yourself. When you're running through those streets and the bulls are coming after you, that's when you really feel it. You run because you'll die if you don't. I'm telling you, that'll clear your mind in an instant.

Danny doesn't move. He listens to the hum of the tyres. In his mind, he can see the bulls coming, all six of them, hurtling down a narrow street. They advance on him as a single unit, a snorting, steaming herd, their hoofs stamping on the cobbles. The horns coming closer and closer. Pamplona, he thinks. He feels the name in his mouth and repeats it a few times, the echo reverberating around his head, like a sigh in three parts.

Pam-plo-na.

He spins the Alfa's rear wheels and says: How far is it to Pamplona?

*

Robert weighs up his words as he answers. It's in the north of Spain, he says, just over the French border. If

I keep on driving and don't stop for too long, I'll get there early tomorrow morning.

They're at the highest point of the bridge now, which has no water underneath it, just another motorway. A few cars and a minibus disappear under the flyover. They descend slowly and see the landscape after the bridge lying flat and green beneath a grey sky.

Do you want to come with me?

That was what he was waiting for. He looks at Robert. He really wants to say yes, right away, but he holds back and manages to say nothing. He keeps quiet and he waits, as you sometimes have to when you want to get results. He slowly opens and closes the Alfa's passenger door, open, closed, open, closed.

Robert says: For a man who doesn't have a specific place in mind, Pamplona is a great destination. Maybe the best destination of all.

Yeah, maybe.

You're welcome to come. If you like.

Pamplona, Danny thinks, flicking the door shut.

If you've got the guts.

Robert takes his foot off the accelerator. Then he presses down again and lets the engine roar.

Danny snorts. It's not about guts, he says.

Yeah, I've heard that one before.

I'll come with you.

Good, says Robert. You'd better put on one of those T-shirts before you get pneumonia.

He points at the bag on the back seat.

Danny struggles out of his wet T-shirt. He slides his arms from the sleeves and drapes the T-shirt over one of the bags. Then he takes a white T-shirt from another bag and puts it on. It's too small for him. The material feels tight around his chest and his upper arms.

Tomorrow we'll be bull runners, says Robert.

Danny nods. He toys with the car door again, pulls it open. There's a snap and he feels the door give way. It comes off and drops onto his lap. He glances over at Robert, who is staring at the car in front. Danny picks up the door and slides it inside the toy car, which he then hides in the glove compartment.

After a while, Robert says: I saw that.

It was an accident.

I know.

Danny doesn't respond. He looks at the boy in the photo and hears Robert say: Don't worry about it. These things happen.

Danny looks at the motorway and clenches his jaw; his head feels heavy and a nerve is twitching in his temples. The snap of the door coming off the little Alfa echoes around his head, along with the sound of his fists pounding the body lying before him, limp and twisted. Hitting the spleen, the liver, again and again, swinging back and hitting again. Now the stomach.

The lanes of the motorway are wedged between concrete noise barriers, which are the same grey as the tops of the buildings rising above them. Robert tells him that the start of the route that the bulls will run tomorrow morning looks just like this, but much narrower, and with no tarmac, of course, and no greenery. An alleyway between high, windowless walls, with cobbles underfoot that are slippery with rain or early-morning dew. Danny stares at the concrete and feels the bulls coming again. After the noise barrier, there's a village. A few houses line the road beyond. Then the landscape is empty for a long time. Danny's head empties too and he feels a little calmer.

Pamplona. He has a goal and someone to take him there. He is on his way. There's nothing to see in the wing mirror now, just the hard shoulder, the crash barrier and the green of the fields.

It's stopped raining. The windscreen wipers are still. They're approaching another bridge. The road is suspended on two enormous white metal arches, with a river flowing beneath, calm and wide. They cross the river and the landscape changes, becoming even more bare, with just the occasional house or a farm with a few outbuildings. They pass a local bus with dirty windows. The driver's the only person on the bus. Robert speeds up, moves into the left-hand lane and overtakes a car. As they drive past, Danny sees a big black dog jump up against the back window. It rests its front paws on the window and barks silently. White slobber flies from the corners of its mouth and drips down the glass. The old man at the wheel keeps his eyes on the road ahead.

The photo on the dashboard glints in the light. Danny leans forward to look at their faces. The little boy's smile is forced and the girl and the woman are scowling into the lens. A word is printed on the plastic of the dashboard just beneath the photograph: *AIRBAG*. There's a Volkswagen in front of them. The VW logo on the back of the car is getting closer. Airbag, he thinks. Again, he tries to imagine the dangers of Pamplona. He tries to picture himself facing the bulls. And suddenly he sees how everything in the car is designed to take Robert safely to Pamplona. And back home again.

*

Music was blaring out of the speakers. As he walked past, he turned his head to escape the noise, but even when he reached the corridor to the changing room the din was still thudding away in his temples. The air was ringing, his ears were ringing. Ron walked beside him. He had slung his nylon hooded gown and towel over his arm and was carrying a sponge bucket and a drinking bottle. He held out the bottle to Danny.

In a minute.

They went around the corner and into the changing room, where Richard was leaning against the wall. Well done, mate, he said.

Danny sat down on the bench.

Four rounds, said Ron, repeating it a couple of times. He put the bucket on the floor and the bottle on the bench, dropped the gown and towel beside it and clapped his hands a few times. Then he started pacing across the changing room from the bench to the door and back.

Four rounds, he said again. He went over to Danny and started to unwrap his hands. His right eyebrow was cut. They'd used something to seal the wound between the second and third rounds, but it had bled pretty badly and he had blood on his gloves, his chest and his shorts. Ron wet the sponge, wrung it out over the bucket and wiped Danny's face. It made the wound sting.

You got any more of that stuff?

Richard shook his head. You'd better get some stitches put in that.

Now?

I'll go and fetch someone who can do it for you, Richard said. He got up and went back to the sports hall.

Danny stood up. His legs had felt heavier after other fights.

You could go another four rounds right now, easy, said Ron, unlacing Danny's boots.

Leave it, said Danny. He sat down against the wall and breathed in deeply.

Someone knocked on the open door. A man in a wheelchair appeared in the doorway. Ron looked up and said: Mr Varon.

Rosenberger Junior.

Everything okay?

Couldn't be better, said the man. Ron walked over to him and they shook hands.

Come on in, said Ron. Congratulations.

The man looked at Danny and said: Yeah, I think congratulations are in order.

He rolled into the changing room, headed straight for Danny, shook his hand and said: Gerard Varon.

The man in the wheelchair had to look up at the other two men, but he was still a formidable presence. It was me who organized all this, he said.

Ron came and stood beside Danny.

That brother of yours wasn't exaggerating.

Ron said: We know what our boys are capable of.

True enough, said Gerard Varon. And so did your dad. Good old Rosenberger.

He was still looking at Danny. They were sitting opposite each other: Danny on the bench, the man in his wheelchair.

I used to have a lot of lads from Rosenberger's. But there weren't many like you.

No, said Ron.

That Bulgarian was no pushover.

He didn't have a cat in hell's chance.

Maybe he was tired from the journey. He only got here yesterday.

Our Danny's still good for another few rounds, said Ron.

Danny listened to their conversation. His heart was thumping. It was thumping harder now than during the fight. He looked at the man, at his grey hair and his coat and the shirt he was wearing underneath it. The collar was long and pointed. Two white patent-leather shoes sat on the wheelchair's metal shelf.

I heard this was your twenty-ninth fight.

That's right.

He's modest, our Danny, said Ron.

But most of them had an early finish.

He doesn't like doing things by halves.

Or are you not keen on counting points?

You could say that, said Danny.

Someone tapped on the door. It was a metallic sound, maybe a ring. A woman with long black hair appeared in the doorway. She looked Asian, Thai perhaps, or Filipino.

Here you are, she said. Her skin was dark, like copper. The make-up around her eyes accentuated them. Green eye shadow.

Gerard turned briefly to look at her and beckoned her in. Then he looked back at Danny and Ron.

This is Ragna, he said. She works for me.

Danny watched her as she came into the changing room. She had long legs and was wearing calf-length trousers. She appeared not to walk but to glide across the floor. When she reached the wheelchair, she stopped. She didn't shake hands. A bag hung over her shoulder and both of her hands stayed firmly on the bag.

Hello, Ron mumbled. Danny did the same.

Ragna's impressed, said Varon. And she knows what she's talking about.

Danny lowered his head and breathed in. Then he sat up straight, pushing his shoulders back against the cold brick wall.

In fact, everyone's impressed, the boxing promoter continued. He signalled to Ragna. She took a slim metal case from her bag, popped it open, slid a card out of it and handed it to the man, who passed it to Ron.

Will you give that to your brother? We should have a chat. Maybe we can work together again.

As the man spoke, he looked at Danny with tired eyes that had dark red veins running through the white.

Thanks, said Ron.

Get him to call me, eh?

I'll pass on the message, Ron replied. Gerard gave him a tight smile. The woman had stepped away from the wheelchair and was running her fingers through her black hair. She was looking either at Danny or at the wall behind him. Her eyes were dark and shining.

I hope to hear from him soon.

The man shook hands with both of them, turned his wheelchair around and rolled himself to the door. As he passed the woman, he placed one hand on her back, and she allowed herself to be guided out into the corridor without saying a word. When they'd gone, Ron said: How about that? I thought he might have something for me.

Danny was breathing heavily.

Richard came back into the changing room. The doctor will be here soon, he said. He looked at his brother, who was waving the business card in the air. What have you got there?

They like the look of Danny, said Ron. He passed the card to his brother. He left this for you.

He was actually here?

Yes.

Varon himself?

Yeah.

Richard stroked his cheek with the card, rasping it against his stubble, and slowly said: Very good. Very good indeed.

Danny didn't say anything.

Richard laughed. Very good, he repeated. And at least that guy pays.

He wants you to call him.

Yeah, very good indeed, said Richard, tucking the card into his pocket. I tell you, this is going to be a great year.

Just as well Dad's not here to see it, Ron replied.

Yeah, Richard agreed. He sniffed and wiped his nose on the back of his hand. Then the future wouldn't look quite so bright, eh?

Danny glanced over at the doorway, where her image was slowly fading.

*

Now that he knows his destination, his thoughts have calmed, appearing one after another as though in a slideshow. He sees the yellow and orange of the slippery floor as a blurred mosaic, liquid, sweat. People all around him. He straightens up. The crowd shrinks back and he takes one last look at the floor, sees an arm lying there, bent and motionless.

Robert lets a Renault overtake. Then he says: So, boxing. Is that much of an earner nowadays?

Depends who you're boxing for.

No idea who you box for. I'm just asking if you can make a good living.

Good enough.

Do you need to have another job?

No.

Do you get paid per fight?

Per drop of sweat. Satisfied?

Robert's gaze passes over Danny's face, over his body, to the car's bonnet. He hugs the steering wheel, pushes back into his seat. The only sound is his finger tapping on the wheel. Danny nods, the smallest of gestures.

Maybe bull running's a bit like boxing, says Robert. But with a whole load of people against a bunch of mad bulls instead of just two men.

Danny shakes his head. Boxing's completely different.

Yeah, sure. But I mean maybe the sensation in your body's the same.

Danny doesn't respond.

How many times have you fought?

About thirty.

Right. So you've been doing it a long time.

A good few years.

Robert overtakes a car. When they're back in the right-hand lane, he says: Why did you stop?

What?

Why did you stop?

I just did, Danny manages to say. He swallows. He hears the sound of the people watching, so close by. A man shouting: Stop. A woman screaming something over and over, her voice so high it could shatter glass. Something falling to the floor with a thud, like a stone, and then bouncing up again before landing and splintering into hundreds of pieces with a smash as clear as the bell between rounds.

You won your last fight, did you?

That's what I said.

I once heard that boxers always give up boxing after they've lost a fight.

Danny stares at the white line between the car and the crash barrier. He doesn't respond.

They pass beneath a flyover and a shadow falls over their faces. When they plunge back into the light, Danny glances over at Robert's twitching lashes. They pass a petrol station with a few cars and caravans in the car park behind the building. Danny tries to work out where they are. They've been driving for less than an hour, but he feels like he's been in the car all day.

He tries to picture Pamplona and the long drive ahead of them, but he has no mental image of the city. His thoughts keep returning to where he came from, to the chaos, to the lights, to the chrome chairs and the small tables, and the blind fury that seized him, fuelled by the sounds all around him. Now that fury is shivering up his spine again, to his neck, to his head. The fury was what made that fight different from all of his previous fights, when he kept his cool and watched and waited, just as he is forced now to wait in the car and to watch the motorway, to keep himself calm.

*

The fly buzzes high up against the back window. It hums and twitches its way along the window towards him, until it settles on the glass and Danny can get a closer look at it. Its head is big and bloated. It drops down and disappears behind his seat.

Mind if I put on some music?

It's your car, says Danny, looking at the radio, at the buttons and the tuner.

Let's see if we can find something decent, says Robert, pressing a button. The radio lights up, the speakers on the parcel shelf crackle. The sound of a guitar and a man singing, applause, cheers slowly becoming quieter and fading away. The music continues.

Haven't heard this one for a long time, says Robert. Our first holiday. We played it the whole time.

The song finishes and a man starts talking. He's rattling on about something he read in the newspaper. For a moment, Danny freezes in his seat. His left

40

hand shoots out and hits the button. The man's voice disappears.

Don't you want the radio on?

Not that crap.

Well, you could have just said.

Robert slides his hands around the steering wheel, nodding his head up and down as though the music's still playing.

That was a good one, says Robert. Now that the music's stopped, he hums the tune to himself.

Danny coughs.

Want some water?

Yeah.

In that bag.

Danny takes the bottle of mineral water out of the grocery bag. Robert says he doesn't have any glasses, so he unscrews the cap and drinks from the bottle. He has another swig, hands Robert the bottle, and then takes the bottle back, screws the cap on and puts the bottle between his feet.

Robert looks over the edge of the steering wheel and hums. He frowns. That was our first holiday, he says. With that music. And with our first car.

Danny isn't listening. Ragna appears in the rear-view mirror. He retreats inside his head and struggles to make sense of what happened. He closes his eyes, sees her lying there on his bed. On a coloured sheet. She's sleeping. The other side of the bed is empty.

The traffic in front of them is slowing down. Robert brakes, joins the vehicles in the right-hand lane, swears a couple of times. They slowly approach a lorry lying on its side in the verge. A red car is parked on the hard shoulder behind the lorry, its door open. A man stands directing the traffic into the left-hand lane. The sounds from outside filter through into the car. Someone shouting. As they get closer, Danny sees chickens all over the road. Hundreds of chickens are huddled together on the tarmac and there are wooden crates all around, with chickens inside. Another man is trying to chase the chickens onto the verge. In one single movement, he kicks two of the birds onto the grass. Then he bends down and flaps his hands to drive the creatures along.

Lucky we can get past, Robert says as he joins the left-hand lane. Damn lucky. The whole motorway'll be clogged up before long. There's going to be a huge tailback.

He sees flashing lights approaching from behind them, moving along the hard shoulder. No siren though – that's just in Danny's head. A police car, followed by a fire engine. The blue lights dance over the toppled lorry, over the feathers and beaks and eyes peering out between the slats of the boxes.

Even when they're past the chicken lorry and driving along in the right-hand lane, the siren's still blaring in Danny's head. The sound slowly changes into a human scream. Danny narrows his eyes and the motorway becomes a thin grey strip. His heart beats faster. He takes a few deep breaths. He can hear the high-pitched sound clearly now. It surrounds him, like the noise of two cats fighting in a courtyard at night.

Danny clenches his fist and winds the material of his white T-shirt around his knuckles, like a hand wrap. He closes his other hand around the white fist and squeezes hard.

*

They pass a town and see a strip of football pitches running alongside the motorway, and a row of flats with glass balconies beyond. Danny looks out at a tower block and a tall structure that could be a radio mast. After the town, they drive past a farmhouse. The smell of chicken shit hangs in an invisible cloud over the motorway. The car battles its way through. As the smell slowly clears, Danny turns his face to the door, looks at the mirror. He remembers the wall of mirrors in the gym at the boxing school, the way they reflected the flash of his eyes as he circled the punch bag, jabbing in rapid combinations. His bandaged fists flashed too, against the leather, which was damp with his sweat.

A small, brightly coloured car overtakes them. A woman is driving; she has long hair and the same colour skin as Ragna. He watches her as the car becomes smaller and smaller and is finally swallowed by the horizon.

Get a good look? says Robert.

Danny doesn't react.

Want me to follow her?

No need.

That was a fine-looking woman though, Robert says, shifting his hands to the bottom of the steering wheel and resting his little fingers on his thighs. He leans one elbow on the door and rubs his chin.

Know what struck me about that lorry?

What?

Those chickens. They just stayed where they were. He pauses. They could have flown away, but they didn't.

Chickens can't fly.

Well, they could have walked away, says Robert. Anyway, they must be able to flap about a bit. Whatever, it just goes to show they're already half-dead. Not like the bulls in Pamplona – they're a completely different story.

Robert sucks on his bottom lip. It makes a squeaking sound.

Danny waits and listens. They're zooming along in the left-hand lane, but it feels as though they're crawling.

Don't you think?

I don't know, says Danny.

The monotone hum of the engine accompanies them on their journey south. Danny's thinking about the bulls, not as Robert sees them, but as he sees them, as a static image.

Do you know what I think? Robert says. Chickens are stupid.

Danny looks straight ahead. The photo on the dashboard becomes larger. The woman and the two children nod at him. He feels like pulling the photo out of the frame and ripping it up.

Robert rests his hand on the gearstick, but doesn't change gear. For a long time, they sit in silence. They cross the border. The motorway curves high above Antwerp. The houses of the city lie in a tangle beneath the road. He spots a gym. Cars jostle around the exits for the city centre, but Danny and Robert stay in the bypass lane, which slowly changes appearance as they drive on, leaving Antwerp behind. Robert says: Sometimes running away is the best thing to do.

Danny glances over at him, at the steering wheel, at the hand casually resting on it. The needle of the speedometer quivers between 120 and 130.

From the bulls, I mean, Robert continues. Running away from the bulls.

Danny wonders whether there are bulls running after him. It feels as though the bulls were released this morning and they've been chasing him all day.

He and Robert exchange a look. When they're both staring ahead at the tarmac again, Robert says: Running away is a natural thing to do. It's survival instinct. A reflex. Those chickens don't have that reflex. They're going to die. Whether they want to or not.

Tall lampposts line the central reservation, their bases thick with grime. Some have seagulls sitting on top. Robert revs the engine. The fields are strips of green and brown, slowly merging into a flickering patchwork. The sky is blue except for a single vapour trail, which spreads wider and wider and then evaporates.

Danny closes his eyes.

*

It was dark and cold and he was lying on his bed, staring up at the dark beams of the attic. He mumbled her name. She answered.

Danny.

Here, he said. He held his cock tight, squeezed it, made it grow. He put his other hand between his legs, tensed his thighs and said her name again. Yes, Danny. He thought of her face, of her eyes, of her dark hair and the way its colour contrasted with the ceiling. He felt her hand around his cock. She stroked it. He slid across the bed towards her, went onto his knees and leant forward. Resting one hand on the top of her head, he whispered something in the darkness. His hand twitched urgently. He swore and growled to himself and when he opened his eyes again all he could see was cold, dark beams and maybe a few puffs of his own breath.

At night she was with him, during the day he was alone, in the evenings he went to the boxing school. A dozen other guys trained there with Ron, including Aaron and the young Russian. He worked to maintain his fitness levels. Lots of skipping and running. Boxing in the ring, going at sixty per cent. Sparring with the amateurs who were preparing for their own fights. For some of the lads, these were their first matches. Danny could tell they were nervous. He talked to them during the training sessions. He was the last to leave the building and he walked home at night through snowy streets.

I've had Varon on the phone, Richard said to him one evening in the canteen after training. I tried every day this week, but he's been in Germany. Finally got through to him tonight.

Well?

It's good news. Fights in Germany, that's what it's all about.

He nodded. Richard gave him the card. He wants to talk to you in person.

Do I have to phone him?

Sooner the better.

Danny thought about her and the man who had put his hand on her back as they left the changing room.

What's stopping you?

He went home. He cooked some spaghetti, watched TV and lay on the bed. He thought about her the whole time and about the man called Varon, with his neatly combed grey hair. In the days that followed, he saw Varon's name everywhere. No photos, just his name. In magazines and newspapers, on a poster for a kickboxing gala stuck to the door of an electricity substation. Even on the radio. The voice that had dominated the changing room after the fight with Hristov now came out of the tiny speakers in his attic. An item about boxing and the criminal world. Was she there too, at the radio station? Did she push him through the studio doors in his wheelchair?

He kept thinking about her, couldn't stop whispering her name. If he could have behaved any differently, he would have done. The nights became carbon copies of each other until one evening a terrible screeching started up outside, between the blocks of flats. It sounded like a baby crying. He went downstairs, pushed open the window in the stairwell, looked down and saw a cat with white patches dart away over the fence of his downstairs neighbours, and a black cat on the roof of a nearby shed. He didn't know if it was the cats or something else, but his mind was clear for the first time in ages. He went back upstairs, turned on the light, searched through the papers on his table. When he found the card, he smoothed out the creases and looked at it for a long time, as though he might discover something in the letters and numbers. A dark coffee stain marked one corner. He put the card down on the table, went to bed and slept well for the first time in weeks. His pillow lay beside him as he fell asleep and when he woke up he was hugging it to his stomach. There was a damp patch on the sheet. He slid out of bed and pulled on his jogging bottoms. The next thing he did was pick up the phone and dial that number. He knew it by heart.

2

Danny opens his eyes and focuses. The crash barrier has gone. There's a strip of grass running along the hard shoulder, with a blackened, scorched-looking edge. In the distance, beyond the ploughed fields lying marshy and heavy in the sunlight, he sees some huge sheds with lorries parked in front. Music is playing very quietly inside the car, French music. He notices a blanket tucked between his left shoulder and the seat. He's been tucked in like a child. He pulls off the blanket and tosses it onto the back seat. The seatbelt's wrapped around his wrist. It hangs loosely across his chest.

Police, says Robert.

Danny's eyes flash. He looks out of the window. Nothing but cars with French number plates.

Where are we?

Just outside Paris.

Danny shakes off the seatbelt. He stretches, turns his head a few times. His neck clicks. He rubs his face and his forehead with the flat of his hand. Paris, he thinks. He asks Robert if he has a map.

I know the route I'm taking.

It's just for me, so I can see where we are.

In there.

Robert points at the glove compartment. Danny pulls the pile of roadmaps from beneath the Dinky toy and looks at them one by one. He opens up a map of France, folds it out onto his lap. The map covers half of the windscreen. Paris is a multicoloured patch with Lens above it, in roughly the area where they must be. There's Lille. And right at the bottom, beside the Atlantic, there's Bordeaux, with the Spanish border beneath it. Pamplona comes after that. It's not on the map. He stares at the coloured paper for a long time, at the wide red-and-yellow line crossing the whole of France, which they'll follow all the way to Bayonne, before falling off the map.

Danny folds the map so that he can look at northern France. He reads the names of the French towns on the road signs and looks for the same names on the map. Slowly Paris comes closer.

Is the music disturbing you?

He listens to the radio for a moment, to a woman's voice. Says no.

Sleep well?

Yes.

Nice dreams?

What?

Look at that blanket.

What about the blanket?

You were drooling all over it.

Danny looks at the map, holds his finger to the paper and tries to concentrate on the place names. His finger is fixed on the middle of Paris, where red lines and yellow lines intersect.

You weren't dreaming about boxing, says Robert.

The map rustles in his hands. Robert overtakes a lorry and blocks of flats appear on the right, bedecked with satellite dishes. It's still a long way to the city centre, but the buildings are already starting to crowd together. They're driving into the sun. He shades his eyes with his hand and scans the uneven horizon, sees nothing but high-rise blocks stretching into the distance.

And you weren't dreaming about your mother either.

Leave my mother out of it.

They carry on driving. After a while, Robert says: I always used to dream about Kim Wilde.

Who?

Kim Wilde. Whenever Kim popped round to visit, my mum had to change the sheets the next morning. It'd either be her or those three girls from Bananarama.

Never heard of them either.

But you were dreaming about someone like that, weren't you? Hair a bit wild, those eyes. You know what I mean.

New cars join the traffic while others disappear into the maze of exits. Robert concentrates on the road. There's a six-storey building beside the motorway. The top two floors on the corner are gutted, the walls are scorched, the window frames charred. On the corner of the building, a melted drainpipe curls away from the wall. Danny folds up the map. He's thinking about her.

He says: Yes, she was certainly wild.

But she isn't wild now?

Danny looks at the map, then back outside.

You said: She *was* wild.

That's right.

Did you dump her?

Danny feels a muscle twitch in his back. He shifts position, puts one hand on the small of his back and loudly exhales.

Or did she dump you?

None of your business.

She dumped you, didn't she?

Danny doesn't reply.

Is that why you're running away? Or doesn't it have anything to do with that?

You fucking heard what I said, didn't you? Danny says, hitting the dashboard with the map.

Robert blinks a few times and says: No need to take it out on the map.

Danny runs his finger around the edge of the map, smoothes out a crease.

That Kim Wilde, says Robert, she's still wild. She doesn't have a choice really, does she? He laughs. Not with that name.

If the map had still been open on his lap, Danny could have buried his face in it. All he can do is shove it into the pocket in the passenger door, close his eyes and hope that Ragna will disappear from his thoughts. But then he pictures her black hair and the contours of her face. And the cold tiled floor.

Slowly, he opens his eyes and focuses on the bustle of Paris. The houses along the motorway have small balconies. He sees a bearded man in a long white robe, leaning on a railing. On another balcony, a moped is standing upside down.

The car's boxed in. Robert stays in the right-hand lane.

That your wife?

Robert fiddles with his earring and gives it a tug. Then he points at the photo on the dashboard and says: Yeah. That's Manuela.

Manuela?

Yes.

And does Manuela look a bit like her?

Like who?

Kim Wilde.

Manuela's my wife, says Robert.

So she doesn't look like her?

At least I got to give my woman a proper goodbye this morning.

Danny snorts. Then he explodes: Like that's my fucking fault.

Robert apologizes.

It's okay, says Danny. He looks at the photo.

Were they already up when you left?

The little ones?

Yes.

I kissed them both and they waved me off. I blew my horn as I was driving away and then gave it another blast when I went round the corner.

His eyes seemed to have calmed down, but then the tic starts again. Danny thinks about the bulls and says: They're sure you'll be coming back?

They wouldn't let me go otherwise.

So Pamplona can't be that dangerous then.

It's not about danger. It's about the way it makes you feel. Inside. Robert bangs his chest with his fist. It's a feeling. Do you understand?

Danny understands. A feeling that rages in his body and his head, a feeling he wants to control.

53

The Eiffel Tower suddenly appears, off to one side. Danny leans forward to get a better view. It seems to be swaying in the wind. Then the tower disappears behind tall buildings. Danny peers along the road to see where it's going to pop up again, but it doesn't reappear.

He looks at the photo on the dashboard, at the hand on the girl's shoulder. He swears to himself. She's not just his wife. She's a mother.

It takes them a long time to get out of Paris, but eventually the buildings become smaller and the kilometres of anonymous industrial estates give way to fields.

He hears Robert's voice again. You known her a long time?

A while, he growls.

Robert is silent. Even the car seems silent. Danny puts his hands in his pockets. They drive in silence down the toll road to the south.

*

The motorway splits at Saint-Arnoult. Robert takes the exit for the first service area and asks Danny if he'd like something to eat. He pulls into a space at the edge of the car park. There are a few lorries at the other end and a man who's checking the straps on his tarpaulin. Then he disappears behind his lorry. They get out of the car. The air's warm and dry. Danny feels the heat of the ground rising up through his shoes, caressing his legs.

Beside the restaurant is a hoarding with a huge advertisement for cigarettes. Danny thinks about cigarettes as they walk to the entrance. Smoking cigarettes. That's what she does in bed at night. She lies on her stomach with her elbows on the pillows. The ashtray in front of her on the edge of the bed. The smoke drifting up into the top of the attic. She stubs out her cigarette and pushes the ashtray away. He remembers the way her eyes looked as she threw the sheet back for him. That wild look.

Robert heads inside, into the smell of coffee.

Danny stops. Just stretch my legs, he says.

He walks around the building until he sees the motorway again, with the car park on the right. The lorries are lined up in one corner. A row of conifers stands between the last lorry and the motorway. Cars thunder past beyond the trees. The air smells of bulls. He crouches down and stares at the ground, at the fine moss growing in the cracks.

You look for something?

Danny turns around. A man is smoking a roll-up beside the cabin of the last lorry.

He shakes his head.

You need a ride?

Already got one.

Danny stands up and when he sees the number plate he says in Dutch: You're from the Netherlands.

Yeah, says the man. And so are you. Where are you heading?

Spain.

Same here, says the man. He slaps the side of the lorry, takes a last drag of his roll-up and stubs it out with his shoe. He nods at the trailer. Danny realizes that the lorry is a cattle transporter. Now he knows where the smell's coming from. Red-and-white cows huddle together behind the planks. He can see a wet nostril through one of the gaps, with a tongue licking away at it.

I'm taking them to be slaughtered.

The sound of the motorway is drowned out by a cow's hoof banging against the side of the lorry. A cow bellows. Between the planks, he sees one big, dark eye with another eye right beside it, belonging to another cow. He senses that the cows aren't standing so close together because the trailer is too small, but because they know what's going to happen to them. And all they have is one another.

The man takes out his tobacco pouch and rolls another cigarette. He says: That abattoir down there, you've never seen anything like it. It's an entire village. They ride bikes to the canteen when they have their break. If they walked, they'd have to leave again as soon as they got there.

He's silent for a moment. The cow bellows again.

Don't I know you from somewhere?

Danny doesn't answer.

From TV or something. We always watch the boxing round at my mate's place.

That's not me.

No, I'm sure I've seen you before.

Got to go, says Danny. He walks towards the motorway, before changing his mind and heading back to the restaurant.

The lorry's engine starts and it begins to move, shuddering and shaking, and lumbers towards the motorway.

Some children are playing by the restaurant entrance. They're climbing on the fence between the pavement and the bushes that surround the building. They take it in turns to jump off the fence and play chicken with the sliding doors, running up to the entrance and then shrieking and darting back to the bushes when the doors open. Then they wait for the doors to swish shut again. As Danny approaches, they sit there on the fence, looking the other way.

Robert's at a table just inside the door, talking to someone on the payphone. Danny goes to the toilets. There's a lorry driver in there, washing his hands. He's younger than Danny and has a pockmarked face. A roll-up hangs from the corner of his mouth. As he holds his hands under the drier, he looks over at Danny. The machine comes to life and starts blowing and whining. Danny disappears behind the door of the cubicle in the far corner. He locks it and waits for the drier to stop. He leans against the tiled wall, tilts his head back. There are damp patches on the ceiling. He sees the tiles of the changing room. He puts the seat down and sits there, his elbows on his knees and his head heavy in his hands. He presses his hands against his temples. It feels as though his head is in a vice that's slowly tightening. His head starts to crack, but the thoughts don't go away.

He stands up, undoes his trousers, clasps his penis in his left hand. He feels small and, as that feeling sinks in, he feels himself shrink even more.

He pisses in the toilet, over the seat. It splashes onto the tiled floor. He takes a few sheets of toilet paper from the holder, wipes the seat, throws the paper into the toilet and flushes. He washes his hands and looks in the mirror. The wall above the mirror is a dingy white. He looks down, holds his hands under the stream of lukewarm water and stares at the mirror, at his hard blue eyes. He shuts them and waits for the water to get colder so he can let it run over his wrists. But the water stays lukewarm.

*

Richard was standing behind the bar in the canteen at the boxing school, his hands resting on the wood. Aaron and three dark-skinned guys, one of them from Cuba, were sitting on the other side of the bar. Ron was propping up the bar beside the Cuban. Rich said the Cuban had been amateur world champion. Ron stood there for a long time, watching the Cuban, listening to him complain about the cold. Then he said in English: You trained in Havana?

Yes, said the Cuban.

With Sanchez? That tall guy?

The Cuban nodded.

The one with the long, thin arms?

Yes. I trained with Sanchez.

Sanchez with the gold earrings? He grabbed hold of his earlobes. In both ears?

Yes, man.

Ron smiled at his brother and said in Dutch: Brother, give me another coffee. And give him something a bit less strong this time. The Sanchez I'm talking about was the porter at our hotel.

The Cuban didn't understand everything Ron said, but he saw the smiling faces of the two brothers and he smiled too. Everyone in Havana is called Sanchez, he said.

Yeah, yeah, said Ron, and we're all called De Vries.

They laughed.

And my brother's supposed to be the stupid one, said Richard. How about that?

He poured out the coffee. As he passed Danny his glass of water, he said: I'm glad you've done it.

Danny looked up. There was a calendar on the wall behind Richard, with a photo of Ron and Richard's dad beneath it, surrounded by a crowd of boxers. A black-and-white photo from the newspaper. *Boxers Conquer Los Angeles*.

Danny said: He didn't seem very friendly.

But you've made an appointment?

Yes.

That's the main thing, said Richard. Yeah, I'm glad you've done it. He ran his hands over the bar.

He didn't say anything else?

He said there'll be time for all that later.

Good, good, Richard said.

Danny looked over at the Cuban and Aaron's mates. They were drinking tea. He turned back to Richard. Will you come with me?

Me? He wanted to talk to you, didn't he?

But it might be about stuff I don't understand.

Richard rubbed his palm across his cheek. Then he clasped both hands over his stomach. So keep your mouth shut and listen. I think he just wants to meet you. To see what you're like.

Danny didn't reply.

If it's about money, tell him to talk to me.

Danny spun round on his stool. The sun was shining on the fronts of the houses over the road. What kind of man is he, this Varon? he asked.

He's a good bloke, said Richard. When he gets an idea in his head, he makes it work. He's that kind of guy. Not a time-waster.

What's wrong with him?

His legs? I don't know. All I know is he's in a wheelchair.

Danny sat in silence for a while.

You've just got to go for it, said Richard. He put his right hand on the bar and wiped the wood. What could go wrong?

*

Danny sits down across from Robert, who still has his ear to the telephone.

Let me speak to the little guy, he says. He waits for a moment, someone says something to him, and then Robert says: Hi, big boy.

A pause.

Or are you a little boy?

Another pause.

Okay then, little boy. Have you read your book?

And another pause.

The book about the cow. That's the one you wanted to read, isn't it? Robert laughs. Daddy's going to see the moo-cows too.

Danny looks over his shoulder at the other tables and

at the bar, where two lorry drivers are sitting. There's a group of men drinking coffee and smoking at the long table in the centre of the room.

Robert holds the phone to his chest. Shall we order? he asks, waving in the direction of the bar. A girl standing by the coffee machine sees his signal. She's wearing a blue short-sleeved shirt and her hair is pinned up. Her arms are dark, like Ragna's. She produces a cigarette from beneath the bar, takes a quick drag, turns her face away from the coffee machine and puffs out a powerful plume of smoke.

The same way Ragna smokes, in bed.

Danny doesn't want a cigarette though. He just wants the smoke that hangs around the bed.

He listens to Robert, who's quietly explaining that he's giving someone a lift. A boxer.

Danny turns away. There's a map of the area on the wall, with castles and wells and churches marked on it. And photos of woods and fields and a campsite by the water.

Qu'est-ce que vous prenez?

The waitress is at their table.

What did she say?

She looks at Danny. *Vous désirez un café?*

What do we want to drink? says Robert. He covers the receiver with his hand and says: *Deux cafés, s'il vous plaît. Vous pourriez nous montrer le menu?*

The girl goes over to the bar and comes back with two menus. She gives him one and puts the other one on the table for Robert.

There's lots of meat on the menu, a few things with fish.

Lasagna. Spaghetti with tomato sauce. T-bone steak.

Robert stands up, inserts a few coins into the slot and carries on talking. Danny stares at the tabletop, at the artificial wood grain. Robert ends his call and says: What do you want to eat?

I don't have any money.

I didn't ask if you had money. I asked what you want to eat.

Whatever. Anything.

Spaghetti?

Danny nods.

I'll go and see if that little sweetheart will sort us out then, says Robert. He walks over to the bar, orders and comes back. No problem, he says. They wait. A while later, the girl brings over two plates of spaghetti and puts a bowl of grated cheese on the table with a spoon in it. Robert unrolls his cutlery from the serviette, looks up at the girl and says: Well, don't you look fine today?

Pardon?

I said: *Merci beaucoup.*

As the girl walks away, Robert leans out from the table and watches her swaying hips. *Bon appétit*, he says. He twirls strands of spaghetti around his fork.

A man comes into the restaurant with a briefcase in his hand. He stops just inside the door, holding it open for two women. A long-haired woman of around thirty and a woman in a skirt, with dark curly hair. Black tights. Painted nails. While the women are choosing a table, the man turns to Robert and Danny and says: *Bon appétit.*

Merci, Robert replies.

The man walks between the tables, nods at the women, says hello to the men at the long table and stops at a seat by the window. Danny watches him.

That's a different class of woman altogether, says Robert. Real ladies. But you know what? I still prefer a tasty young bit of stuff.

The man takes some papers from his briefcase and puts them on the table.

Either that or Kim Wilde, says Robert. She must be about fifty now, but that doesn't matter when you're Kim Wilde.

Danny doesn't say anything.

Why are you staring at that guy?

He reminds me of someone.

*

He walked from the tram stop down a road with wide pavements. Past tall buildings. The street ended at a canal. He could see his breath in the cold air. Some men were standing on the opposite pavement outside a building with a tiled facade. They all had beards. Down the road, two girls were sitting together in a doorway, huddled into their coats, sharing a cigarette. He was getting closer to the right house number. When he reached it, he saw a gold plate on the wall with the promoter's name on it. He rang the bell. A few moments later, someone pulled the cord, the lock clicked and the door slowly opened. Varon's voice called down from upstairs. Come on up.

A big hallway and a wide staircase with a chairlift. Danny climbed the stairs to the first floor. He looked at the hat stand. Her coat wasn't there. He went through the open door, walked into the office and found Varon sitting at a long table set at right angles to the wall. He went over and shook his hand.

Hello, Mr Varon.

Please call me Gerard.

Gerard.

Sit down. You're lucky I'm still here. Haven't legged it to Germany yet. He smiled. Get it? Legged it. He slapped his leg and laughed again.

Danny took off his coat, hung it over the back of the chair and sat down opposite Varon. On the other end of the table, there was a telephone with piles of paper beside it. Framed photos hung on the wall. Boxers with their arms in the air. A black guy holding up a huge championship belt. A colour photograph of a giant of a man punching another boxer on the cheekbone. There was no other desk in the office and nothing to indicate that she worked there.

What would you like to drink?

Whatever you've got.

Tea, he said.

Fine.

Gerard rolled his wheelchair to the kitchen. Danny heard the tap running. There was a sound of rattling cups and he called through to Danny: So you want to go for it?

Danny looked over his shoulder at the glistening canal outside. The sun was shining through the balcony doors. It was so hot in the room. A bunch of keys and a shoulder bag lay on a low table. They must be hers.

Gerard came back with a tray on his lap. I've already spoken to one of the Rosenbergers, he said.

Ron?

No, the other one.

Richard. He's not a trainer.

Doesn't matter, Gerard replied. He said you were good. But I already knew that.

Gerard poured the tea. It was steaming hot. He slid one cup across the table, picked up the other and said: I'll keep it brief. I want you on board.

Yes, Mr Varon.

Gerard.

Okay.

In Germany, he continued. I'm working on a new series of fights, at a bigger location, in Leipzig. I need good people. People with commitment. People like you.

He sipped his tea and looked Danny in the eyes. Then he gave him a tight smile that Danny would often remember later. He thought Varon would go on to say something about boxing, but he didn't. He just pointed at the teacups. You want something to go with the tea?

No, thank you.

He drank some tea. It was hot. It burned his mouth, but he didn't let it show.

I think you've got it. Commitment. You're willing to go for it.

I like training.

Yeah, Rosenberger said you did.

When's the fight?

It's a series.

When's the first one?

In the summer. It runs through the autumn, until the end of November. Crowd of twelve thousand. If it's a full house.

Right.

Interested?

And the opponents?

Strong. Are you still in the same weight class?

Yes.

You're not a light heavyweight?

No, I'm well beneath that.

Good. Will you keep up the training until then? I mean, maintain your condition, don't get too heavy.

Yes.

There's still about five months to go. We've got time.

Can I still train with the brothers?

I don't interfere with training. I assume you know what you need to do. You got good people at the Rosenbergers?

Yes.

Then we're done, I think.

Danny nodded. Gerard turned his chair a little, leafed through the papers, took out two sheets, glanced at them and passed them to Danny. It's all in there. Take your time to look through everything. If you leave the papers at the boxing school, I'll send Ragna round to pick them up.

Fine, he said quietly.

I'm going to have a cognac, said Gerard. Think it's allowed, with this bloody cold weather. And there I was, thinking it was almost spring.

He took a bottle and a glass from the sideboard. He poured himself one and looked at Danny.

Just water for me.

He handed Danny a bottle of sparkling water. They clinked. Gerard swirled the cognac around his glass before taking a swig and rolling it around his mouth. Then he looked at the papers and the telephone and said he had to get back to work. Danny stood up, drank some of the water, put on his coat, folded the papers in half, slipped them into his inside pocket and shook Varon's hand.

I'll find my own way out.

If you need anything or you want to talk again, just call.

Thanks.

Danny closed the door behind him and stood on the stairs for a moment. The hat stand was just the same as before. There wasn't a sound to be heard in the house. He went down the stairs, stepped outside and started to walk over to the water, but then stopped on the pavement. There was a lamppost in front of the house and a big green American car in the parking space. A Dodge. He walked past the tall windows and saw himself reflected in the glass. He'd been planning to walk back to the tram stop but changed his mind. He followed the canal until he reached a bridge, which he crossed and then headed back along the other side of the water. He sat down on a yellow kerbstone opposite the Dodge and stared at the house for a long time.

*

Robert slurps up strands of spaghetti. When the plate's empty, he wipes his mouth with the back of his hand, pushes the plate away and leans back. I thought boxers ate loads, he said, nodding at Danny's plate.

Not hungry.

Want me to get a doggy bag?

Robert waves at the bar and the girl comes over to their table. The smell of cigarettes follows in her wake, stronger than before. Robert asks her to pack up the food for them. He calls her *ma chérie*. She nods and asks if they want anything else. Robert says: *Café pour moi*. What about you?

Yeah, same for me.

Deux cafés, s'il vous plaît.

The girl leaves, taking the plates with her.

Robert says: We'll just have our coffee and then we'll be off. Or do you want to use the phone too?

Robert takes some money from his pocket and puts it on the table.

No need.

Robert taps the cord of the payphone. It curls up and twitches.

It'll be a long time before I make another stop.

I told you I don't need to use the phone.

The girl comes over with the coffee pot. As she pours, she looks at Danny. The black coffee swirls around the pot. She leaves. Robert drinks with quick, little sips. Danny presses the hot cup to his cheek.

Are you coming? Robert asks when they've finished their coffee.

Yes.

I'll just get the doggy bag. Robert takes the cups over to the bar and comes back holding a bag. They walk out to the car park. The sun is beating down and a smell of

68

diesel hangs in the air. They get into the car and drive over to the petrol station next to the restaurant. Robert fills the tank, goes inside to pay. When he gets back to the car, he checks the petrol cap, climbs in, starts the engine, turns on the radio and heads back onto the motorway. Danny allows himself to be carried away, deeper into France, to the Spanish border, to Pamplona.

They glide along beneath roads that hang above the motorway, high and narrow. A man is standing on one of the bridges. He leans over the parapet and Danny expects him to spit down on them, but nothing happens as they pass beneath. The clock on the dashboard changes, from minute to minute. He watches and waits for the hour to change.

Robert scratches his arm. He nods at the photo on the dashboard. We'll have been married ten years next year.

The wing mirror glints. Danny looks at the photo, which is also gleaming. Ten years, he echoes.

Yeah, it's a long time. A man can get up to all sorts in ten years, but what you have at home, that's always the foundation. Your rock. That's what you work for. Hey, I'm not making you feel uncomfortable, am I?

It could all change in a moment.

Yeah? Well, let's just assume it won't.

What if one of those bulls charges at you?

That's not going to happen.

You could slip and fall, says Danny.

Maybe, Robert whispers.

A sports car overtakes them with a roar. The pitch changes, high to low, and the car rapidly disappears from sight.

What about you? Robert blinks.

What?

Do you want to go back?

Danny shrugs.

Is it all still too fresh?

Yes.

Too fresh to talk about?

Danny doesn't react.

How did you meet?

Danny moves his left hand to the handbrake, wraps his fingers around it, puts his thumb on the button.

If you ask me one more question, I'm going to stop the car.

Robert keeps his hands on the steering wheel. Danny holds his breath. He squeezes the button on the handbrake and Robert holds his breath too and everything is silent. They drive like that for a few hundred metres. There's a buzzing in Danny's head. He thinks about the night he first saw her, after he beat Hristov. He thinks about the glistening canal. He thinks about the time she came to see him at the boxing school. He waits for Robert to knock his hand away, but Robert's hands stay on the steering wheel.

Without looking over at him, Robert says: You're not going to do that.

They breathe again. Danny lets go of the handbrake and stares at the clock. The two dots are blinking. He waits for the numbers to change and says: She had someone else.

Another man?

He nods.

Danny clenches his jaw. There's an enormous shed beside the motorway with loading bays for lorries, a number above every door. Danny counts. One, two, three, four, five, six, seven, eight.

*

He walked into the gym, stopped for a moment outside the double doors and listened to the familiar sounds. Then he opened one of the doors and looked inside. He saw three boxers doing exercises in the far corner. The tallest one, a slim Moroccan, was jabbing at a punch bag, fast and strong. Another Moroccan and a stocky guy with narrow sideburns were watching. Aaron was sitting on a bench around the corner by the door. He was supposed to be giving fitness training to the juniors, but no one was there.

Where are they all?

Exams.

How long's that for?

Just this week, I think, said Aaron. But you know who was just here?

Who?

Sando. He's been in Curaçao. With one of those women of his.

Curaçao? Wow.

Been there since New Year. She paid for the whole thing.

He's doing well for himself.

You reckon? He said he more or less had to run away from the old hag. She wanted to keep him there.

And he had to give her a good seeing-to every single bloody day. He looked wrecked.

Danny went to the changing room, put on his shorts and his boots, wrapped bandages around his hands and took the gloves out of his bag. He started with skipping. When the other seniors got there, the whole group played a kind of rugby game with the medicine ball. After that, they put on head protectors and gloves and trained in pairs. Every time the bell went between the training sessions, he looked out at the tiled corridor. As he skipped, he kept looking to see if she was coming. After half an hour of training, he heard a voice call his name.

Someone here for you.

He stopped, held the punch bag still. She was standing by the notice board. Aaron walked over and looked out into the corridor. Ah, I see, he said.

She was wearing jeans and a white blouse underneath a padded jacket. Her hair was up.

Back in a minute.

Me too, Aaron said and he spat out his mouth guard.

You're staying here, said Danny.

Aaron picked up the mouth guard from the floor and said: Just need to rinse this off.

You can do that later. I know you and your old boxing tricks.

He headed up the steps and walked over to her. He wriggled his right hand out of his glove, ran his fingers through his hair, wiped his hand on his T-shirt and shook hers.

You here to see me?

I've come to pick up your contract.

It's around here somewhere.

He pointed at the canteen, walked past her and, as he did so, inhaled her scent. The scent of peaches. He took off his other glove and walked over to the open door. Ragna followed him. Even though there was no one in the canteen, the television in the corner was on.

I just thought I'd pop in, see if it was ready, she said.

That's fine, said Danny. It's pretty quiet.

He walked around the bar, looked in one of the boxes above the coffee machine, took out a pile of papers, flicked through them and found his contract. It was in a yellow envelope, which had already been sealed and had the boxing promoter's name and address written on it in blue ink.

See, it was all ready, he said, handing her the envelope.

Was everything okay?

Yes.

We don't just work with professionals, she said. We're professionals ourselves.

Danny nodded. Would you like something to drink?

If you have time.

Sure. Coffee or tea?

Tea, please.

Ragna sat down at a table. Danny made her a cup of tea and poured a large glass of water for himself. Then he went to join her.

I've seen you fight, she said.

I know.

Have you always trained here?

Yeah, for years.

That's what he said. Mr Varon, I mean. He's told me a lot about you. How's your eye now?

Good.

It bled a lot, didn't it?

Looked worse than it was.

She picked up the envelope, turned it over, put it down again and looked at him. He was a head taller, so she had to lift her chin. She said: I don't like watching, you know. Watching people fight. Or shouldn't I be saying that to you?

You can say whatever you like.

She took her cup, stood up and looked at the photos on the wall.

Who's that? she asked.

That's Sando.

She nodded. Are you in the pictures too?

He pointed out a colour photo of himself, standing with ten or so black guys in front of the boxing school. It was a good picture of him. Ragna looked at the photos and sipped her tea.

The outside door rattled and Richard Rosenberger walked into his boxing school.

Danny said: Rich, this is Ragna.

They shook hands.

Our German connection, Richard said with a smile. That's where the money is. But you know all about that. He turned to Danny. Who else is in today?

The Moroccans. And Aaron. And that kickboxer.

Okay, said Richard. He said goodbye to Ragna and headed out into the corridor.

She picked up the envelope, put her cup on the table and turned to Danny. When do you want to step up the training?

Couple of months. Going to build it up slowly.

Do you want to do it here?

Yeah, I'd like to.

During the day?

Yes, that's fine.

With people from here?

He shook his head. They're not here during the day.

Do you want to work with one of our guys?

Sounds good.

I'll send someone round. I hope Pavel's free. He's good. And you'll carry on training as usual in the evenings?

Yeah. I'll ask Ron if he can come in a bit earlier.

Perfect.

They looked at each other for a moment. He tried to force himself not to look away, but his gaze moved to her lips, then down to the table.

I should get going.

I'll come out with you, he said, and they headed outside. Ragna unlocked her bike, put the envelope in her inside pocket, smiled and shook hands with Danny. Then she waited for a man who was pushing his bike along the pavement to go past. There was a small child sitting in a seat attached to the handlebars and a slightly older boy balanced on the back. A ball was jammed under the saddle and the older boy was holding onto it with both hands. The man slowly pushed the bike past the gym and Ragna got on her bike and raised her hand. Danny watched her cycle off down the pavement and around the corner.

*

They are approaching a petrol station. Danny leans forward to read the sign that says how far the next petrol station is. A thought flashes through his mind: grab the wheel, take the exit, call her. So she can tell him everything's okay and he can keep repeating that it was all a mistake, a misunderstanding. That he's sorry. But the thought of her paralyses him. A road lined with trees runs parallel to the motorway. The trees slice the sunlight into fragments that dance over the fields. Danny closes his eyes. Her dark eyes appear in the blackness. They study him calmly, as though she too is apologizing.

He turns away, opens his eyes. Outside there's nothing but fields. The sunlight tingles on his cheek. He rests his forehead on the window, which is surprisingly cool.

Can I ask you something? says Robert. When can you tell that you're going to win?

Really early on.

Right at the beginning of a fight?

Yes.

And when you're going to lose? Can you tell that just as quickly?

No, that's not something you can feel, says Danny.

Robert's silent for a moment, then says: I guess that's something you can only feel when you're standing out in the rain like a drowned rat.

The words hit him hard. His flight through the city streets flashes through his head. Just for a moment, he feels that power again, the power he'd had during the fight. His silent fury. His jabs hitting home. Hard and accurate.

Is that why you stopped for me?

That's not what I mean.

Because you felt sorry for me?

I thought maybe I could help.

Danny doesn't take the bait. He wipes his nose with the back of his hand. A flock of starlings swirls over the cornfields, a dark patch against the sky, constantly changing shape, growing larger, then shrinking. The occasional starling splits off from the group. Danny tries to follow the bird with his eyes, even after the group swallows it up and it disappears, just like the stray thoughts that break away and whirl through the air before merging again with the darkness in his mind.

Tomorrow Pamplona, he hears Robert say. And, after a short silence, he adds: Don't forget Pamplona.

Robert blinks. Danny looks down at his hands on his lap, large and flat, his thumbs between his thighs. He breathes in deeply and the T-shirt tightens around his chest. The white of the shirt hurts his eyes. I won't forget Pamplona, he says.

In the west, the horizon turns red, stripes of colour fill the sky and small clouds dissolve in the last of the light. The cars in front have turned on their headlights. On the other side of the crash barrier, white and yellow lights are coming towards them.

3

Under an ink-black sky, Danny and Robert sit at a picnic table beside a river. The car is parked a short distance away, its back end facing the table.

They drove all through the evening. Robert phoned his wife to say good night from a petrol station just outside Bordeaux. They left the motorway at Bayonne around midnight and Robert drove inland down a narrow road. When Danny wound down his window, he could smell the sea. It took them at least another fifteen minutes to reach the spot by the river, which Robert said was called the Adour. He told Danny he'd often stopped there on his way to Pamplona. To have a rest and a drink, to light a fire and look at the stars.

A strip of grass lies between them and the water. Beyond the grass, pebbles. The river's not wide and it flows along gently. Robert has gathered wood and made a fire in the dip beside the picnic table. The flames dance gently in the breeze. On the table is a jar with a candle in it, which Robert produced from one of his bags. Danny looks at the dark sky above the opposite bank. Stars shine above the rippling water, their reflections rocking on the waves.

Want a drink?

Danny shakes his head.

Of course you want a drink. Something to eat? How about the pasta the waitress packed up for us?

Robert walks over to the car and comes back with a bag. He takes out two bottles and puts them on the table. Whisky and cognac. Then he produces a big bottle of soda water and says: A good drink and Pamplona go together. Like a fire and a beautiful starry sky.

Small blue flames climb up a piece of wood, rising into the dark night sky. Robert twists the cap of the whisky bottle, pours two measures and adds soda water. The gurgle of the whisky echoes above the babbling of the river. Danny catches the scent of alcohol. Robert presses a cup into his hand. Danny waits for him to say cheers, but he doesn't. They drink. The soda water fizzes in his mouth; bubbles and alcohol rise up into his head.

Robert says: What's he like?

Danny puts his cup down on the table. Who?

The other man.

Danny makes circles on the table with his cup. Then he downs his whisky and says: What do you think? He's a filthy son-of-a-bitch.

Robert blinks as he takes a swig and swills it around his mouth. The wind's getting up. I'm a bit chilly, he says. How about you?

I'm okay.

Robert stands up. Did you bring anything with you? A coat? A jumper?

No, nothing.

Robert fetches a coat and a thick woollen jumper from the car and passes the jumper to Danny. Danny puts it down on the bench. One sleeve dangles into the grass. Robert walks over to the fire, adds a couple of pieces of wood and pokes the fire with a long branch. The flames flicker. The smoke drifts to the riverbank, then travels inland, against the current.

I could do with a cigarette though, Danny says.

Can't help you with that.

She smokes in bed, he says. He can picture her lying on the bed in a rectangle of white moonlight, holding her cigarette up at shoulder height. He's sitting at the foot of the bed, leaning against the slope of the wall. One hand on her ankle. She's smoking very deliberately, as if in slow motion. If he'd been sitting to one side, he could have seen her thoughts as they crossed her face in the mirror. Then things would never have gone so far. But he couldn't see her face. And all he could feel was the soft skin above her ankle as he stroked it.

Think that's what she's doing now?

No, says Danny. That's not what she's doing now.

And what about you? What do you do when she's smoking?

I watch her.

*

Two small lights glide over the water in the distance, beyond the bridge. A yellow light and a white one. Torches. He watches until they disappear and the water is dark again.

Take a look up there, says Robert.

Danny looks. Hundreds of stars are shining in the sky. There's no moon.

See that? Robert says. Beautiful. That kind of sight leaves me speechless.

Danny nods.

I reckon just about everything leaves you speechless, says Robert.

Robert pours another one, passes Danny his cup and they drink. I'm going to take a leak, Robert says. He walks over to the long grass. Danny opens the bag, takes out the plastic cutlery, opens the cardboard box. As he twirls the fork in the cold strands of spaghetti and slowly starts eating, he watches Robert hitch up his trousers and walk a short way down the road. He puts his hands on his hips and looks up at the sky. Danny sits there, elbows resting on the table. Then Robert comes back and sits down. He runs his tongue around his mouth, sticks out his bottom lip and says: This spot reminds me of the canal behind our house where we go fishing.

Fishing, Danny repeats quietly.

Yeah. I go fishing with my kids every Saturday. You should see them when they get a bite. When the float starts to twitch and when it goes under, and afterwards, when they're reeling in the fish. They're scared to death of touching the fish. Just a tiny little roach. Absolutely petrifies them. But still, the next Saturday comes around and they want to do it all over again.

A duck quacks in the distance. The sound echoes over the water and dies away. Danny takes a swig.

I can only really remember one time, Robert says, when I felt that kind of fear. That was when they were born.

Robert plays with the jar with the candle inside. He taps the glass and the flame quivers.

That's another thing you can't imagine, he says. It's something you have to experience for yourself. Do you know what the problem is with childbirth? You can't do a bloody thing. As a man, you can be there with her, but there's sod all you can actually do.

He's silent for a moment.

Or don't you believe me?

I believe you.

Doesn't matter. It's impossible if you've never been there yourself. You don't know what's hit you. A hundred bulls don't even compare.

He picks up the bottle, holds it in his hand.

So you just stand there looking. Well, that's what I did. I didn't have a clue what to do. With the first one, I held her hand, because I thought that's what I was supposed to do, and I patted her shoulder a bit. I kept on saying: You can do it, you can do it. Until finally she screamed at me to shut up. With the second one, I just sat by the bed and kept my mouth shut. I thought it'd go more quickly the second time, but there was a problem and it took over twenty-six hours. All that time, you're just sitting there. And you know what? You'd rather be facing the bulls. At least then you know what you're dealing with. When you're sitting there by the bed like that, you might as well be invisible.

Danny leans forward. His forehead comes to rest against his cup. It feels hard and cold and comforting.

Robert holds up the bottle. Danny shakes his head and says: I'm going for a walk.

*

The river lay hidden in the mist. He ran along the water at his normal speed, up to the bridge, and used the steps beside the bridge for some fartlek training. The lampposts on the bridge poked their heads up into the clouds. When he reached the other side, he followed the cycle path between houseboats and a busy street. His breath steamed. A woman came towards him on a bike. As she rode up onto the pavement, she smiled at him. He ran for over three quarters of an hour, at around eighty per cent. When he got back, he went inside, swapped his running shoes for his boxing boots, took his rope from the cupboard, put on his Walkman and started skipping. Even though he was alone, he kept to his usual corner. He listened to the music as the rope swished past his face. The cassette lasted thirty minutes. The Walkman clicked and he stopped, went to the changing room and drank water from the tap.

A man in a checked shirt was standing in the corridor.

Danny?

Yeah, that's me. You Pavel?

Yes.

They shook hands.

Do you speak Dutch?

I'm learning. You ready to start?

Just having a bit of a rest.

Half hour?

Fine, Danny replied.

Pavel was a thick-set man in his forties. He had deep wrinkles in his face, like seams. Pavel got changed into his training gear and Danny put his gloves on. At three o'clock, they started training in the gym. Pavel stayed in the centre and Danny moved around him. They did some interval work, with series of three jabs, as quick as Danny could. Pavel counted. He didn't blink once. He made attacking moves with the pads, something Ron never did. And every time he hit Danny, just a gentle tap, he said: Take it and move on. But first, you've got to take it.

Half an hour went by. Then they repeated the exercise, this time with series of four jabs, culminating in an attack on the punch bag, the bag hovering at an angle under Danny's rapid blows. When they were done, they walked to the changing room.

So where did you train, Pavel?

I don't have any fixed place.

Danny nodded. Do you do much work for Varon?

Now and then. What about you? Who do you normally train with?

Ron Rosenberger.

The big guy?

Yeah.

Any good?

Very.

What does he think of this? Me training you here?

It's not his call.

Good.

Do you like working for him? Danny said.

Yes. He's good at what he does.

How many people work there?

What do you mean?

Other than the two of them.

No one else, said Pavel.

Danny looked at his face, at his eyes, but he couldn't find any clues there.

Danny put on a fresh pair of trousers and a clean shirt. Pavel pulled a checked shirt over the sweater he'd been training in. There was a motorcycle helmet on the bench with his things.

July, wasn't it?

That's when it starts.

Then we've got enough time.

They left the changing room.

Do you know who you're up against?

No.

I've heard there's an Argentinean guy coming over, said Pavel. Ramos. He's in your weight class.

Ramos. You ever seen him fight?

Yes.

And?

Good boxer. Strong. Saw him once back home in Bratislava. He was boxing against a friend of mine.

And Ramos won?

How did you know that?

I can see it in your face.

They went outside. Pavel had parked his motorbike on the pavement beside the boxing school. As Danny looked down the street towards the crossing, he heard the engine revving. A thunderous roar filled the air – the whole neighbourhood must have heard it. The motorbike moved off down the pavement, slowly at first, but then speeding up and rounding the corner with an incredible din.

*

He walks down the tarmac to the bridge, which hangs suspended high above the water, a strange grey arch against the starry sky. The road takes a long curve and Danny climbs up a steep path worn into the grass, with ferns on either side. At the top, he pulls himself over the railing and stands in the middle of the bridge. There's a campsite on the other side. Silhouettes of tents and caravans run down to the riverbank. Lights are on in a few of the tents and he can see shadows moving around inside them.

He goes down to the riverbank opposite the campsite, where the water babbles softly. Downstream, it foams and hisses over the stones. He walks over rough pebbles to the bank and sits down on a big rock. He sits there for a long time, just watching and listening. Then he hears a sound on the other side of the water. Feet crunching on pebbles. Against the backdrop of the tents and the caravans, he can see a fragile figure. A woman. She has a bath towel around her shoulders. She's walking gingerly, in a straight line, down to the water. Her back is bent. When she reaches the river, she lays the towel on the stones. She puts on a swimming cap and walks into the water, still tucking long strands of hair into her cap. After just a couple of steps, the water comes up to her knees. She bends down, splashes it onto her arms and chest, takes another few steps and plunges into the water. She swims into the darkness and soon reaches the middle of the river. Her swimming cap bobs on the water, a patch of grey. She turns onto her back and swims against the current, stays floating in almost the same spot. Hands at her sides, her legs kicking slowly, confidently.

After a while, the woman turns onto her stomach and swims in his direction. She reaches the riverbank with just a few powerful strokes. She rises up out of the water and steps over the shingle, keeping the same calm pace, heading for the rock. When she sees him, she stops.

Je ne t'avais pas vu, she says.

Pardon?

Tu ne parles pas français?

No.

Anglais?

Yes, he says, standing up.

Non, non, the woman says. She gestures that he should stay where he is, but Danny steps away from the rock and says in English: Sit down. Please. He points at the rock. The woman hesitates and then sits down.

Merci.

Only now does he notice how old and frail and thin her legs are. There are flowers in the pattern on her swimsuit.

I swim every night, she says. Now that they've exchanged a few words, she's speaking more slowly. She has to think about her English. She brings her hands together in front of her chest and then holds them to her cheeks.

He crouches beside her, his eyes fixed on the river.

Always this late?

Oui. In the dark, before I go to sleep.

Aren't you cold?

Oh, no. I always have a little rest here. I watch the river and after a while I go back. The river is beautiful at night. Calm.

He nods.

You can think, she says. When you sit here, you can think.

He nods again.

I have a little house there, on the other side. I come here every summer. Forty years now.

Forty years, he thinks.

She dries her legs. And I still swim. I hope I can keep on swimming for a long time.

Hmm.

Are you staying at the campsite?

No. We're just stopping for the night.

Are you here with your girlfriend?

In spite of the darkness, he can make out her eyes. Lively old eyes that gleam in the faint light of the stars. He shakes his head. The woman looks at him and he can tell from the way she says she's sorry that she knows his girlfriend is no longer his girlfriend.

She looks at the water and smiles, a smile meant only for herself.

I met the love of my life in this place.

At the campsite?

Non. Here by the river. The woman shivers. She places her hands on the rock. I was swimming and he walked by. That's how we met. What about you? Who are you travelling with? A friend?

He hesitates for a moment. Yes.

That's good.

He nods.

Nice speaking to you.

She stands up and walks back to the water.

What about your husband? Is he here too?

She turns around, takes a step towards him and says: No, he's not. He was my first love, a whole summer long, but after that summer he went back to Paris. That's where he lived. I never saw him again.

Never?

Never. Not a letter, not a postcard. Nothing. But I return here every year.

Her eyes sparkle against the dark sky, as though there's moonlight reflected in them, but there is no moon. Her eyes are sparkling all by themselves.

She says good night to him and walks to the water. He hears the quiet splashing of her feet. She lowers herself into the water, calmly swims to the opposite bank, steps out of the river, crosses the shingle to her towel and walks through the dark campsite with it wrapped around her shoulders. Her shadow disappears among the tents.

He sits there for a long time, listening to the gentle gurgling of the river. For a moment, he thinks he can hear the sound of the swimmer, but the river is dark and empty. He stands up and looks at the rock. He bends down, puts his hands around it, shifts them, wraps his forearms around the rock and tries to lift it. It doesn't budge.

*

On the way back, the bridge proves an obstacle. When he gets to the top, he looks down the river to where Robert should be. He can't see anything, not even the glow of the fire. He walks along the parapet and, when he spots the path between the dark ferns, he climbs over the railing and heads back down. Long grass brushes against his trousers. He reaches the road and sees two headlights approaching. He lets the car go by and then starts walking along the tarmac. Before long, he reaches the picnic table. The fire's died down to an orange glow, hidden in the earth. Robert's sitting with his back against the table, his legs out in front of him. When he hears Danny, he turns around.

You've been gone a while.

Danny sits down in the same place as before. Beside the jumper. He can smell fish. There are two tins on the table. One of them is open, its lid bent upwards. A small fork is sticking up out of it. The tin opener is lying beside a piece of baguette.

Robert turns around, pushes a cup over to him. Danny drinks. The whisky takes his breath away.

Someone was out there swimming, he says.

At this time of night?

Yes, a woman.

That's why you were gone so long. Robert says with a laugh. Peeping Tom.

It was an old woman.

That doesn't matter, says Robert. Kim Wilde's getting on a bit too.

It wasn't her.

No, that'd be something, eh?

It was a French woman.

Ah, *une française*.

Yeah, whatever.

Robert pushes the open tin to the middle of the table. Want some fish?

Tuna in tomato sauce. Danny identifies a pea in the mush. No, he says.

Robert picks up the tin, has a few mouthfuls, and puts the fork down on the table. He shakes his head and chuckles: Kim Wilde. She really was something.

Danny nods.

You ever seen the video for 'Cambodia'?

Don't think so.

It begins with her tossing around in bed and, if that's not enough, she goes off and starts crawling through the jungle. That bit's really great. She's down on the ground and she just keeps looking at you. With those eyes, you know.

Danny looks at him.

Robert laughs. That was a really great video.

Really great, Danny echoes coolly. He thinks about her and he thinks about Cambodia.

They sit there for a while and a dog comes running up to the table. It sniffs at Robert's leg.

Sod off, he says, pushing the dog away.

The dog walks around the picnic table to Danny, who holds out his hand. It's a big old black sheepdog with a friendly face. It pushes its shoulder against Danny's leg and licks his hand. Robert watches. Can't stand them, he says. Dogs. Specially not big ones like that.

The dog lies down in the grass at Danny's feet. He strokes the dog's head and its back and as he runs his hand through the long fur he looks at the road to see if the dog's owner is coming. He can't see or hear anything. He strokes the dog. Its stomach is warm and its legs are wet. It's been in the river. He talks to it quietly.

It's a French dog, says Robert. It can't understand a word you're saying.

Dogs understand everything.

Robert bends down and looks under the table at the dog. Seems to like it here, he says. I don't know what it is with these creatures, but they're so dumb. It's humans who have made them that way.

They need people.

Exactly, says Robert.

Danny rubs the dog's head.

And obedient, says Robert. I think that's what gets me the most. They're so damned obedient. Chasing after balls, fetching sticks.

He gave you a fright though, didn't he? Suddenly standing there beside you.

Don't you speak too soon. Let's see what you do when those bulls are coming.

The dog hears something. It lifts its head and then lies back down.

Dozy creature, Robert mumbles. He scratches behind his ear and his earring twitches and gleams dimly in the candlelight.

In the distance, they hear a man shout something in French. The dog sits and pricks up its ears. The voice shouts again in the distance. Danny looks at the river, but there's nothing to see. He pats the dog and says: Go on. Go and find your owner.

Another shout and Danny taps the dog on the back. It walks towards the river, disappearing into the darkness. Soon he hears it barking and, a little later, there's a series of gunshots.

Hunters, says Robert. He spits on the grass. Getting

a dog to do their dirty work, he says. It's cruelty to animals.

You go fishing, don't you?

Not with a gun.

Danny expects to hear more gunshots, but the night is silent. It's colder now. He pulls over the jar with the candle in it, cradles it in his hands.

Why don't you put on that jumper?

Danny takes the jumper and pulls it over his head. It has a big collar with a zip. He does up the zip and folds down the collar. Robert blinks and nods approvingly.

*

He was standing at the door of the boxing school, waiting for Ron. He watched the cars and bicycles passing the building and the people walking along the pavement on the other side of the road. He stood at the door for a long time. He paced to the corner of the building and back again. Ron came down the street and raised his hand. He was carrying a sports bag in his other hand.

Thought you'd be here earlier.

Yeah, that was the idea.

Lot of traffic?

Yeah, that was it.

They headed inside and got changed. Danny opened the door for Ron and they walked to the lockers together. They said hello to a young trainer called Khalid, who was working with a group of boys. All of the children had dark hair except for one red-headed boy. They were standing in a row with their fists up to their faces. The boys all looked over at Danny.

Hey, I'm over here, said Khalid. The boys looked back at their trainer. Ron went over to the punch bag in the far corner, put his hand on it, gave it a gentle push, waited for it to swing back and said: Just the usual routine, mate?

They warmed up and Danny did the same exercises he'd done with Pavel, but not as many and not at the same pace. Halfway through the session, he looked at Ron. Ron nodded to say that everything was fine.

After an hour, they sat down on the bench for a rest. The boys had got changed and then stood in the doorway watching for a while. Now they shyly came down the steps towards Danny.

Are you fighting in another competition? asked a boy with short dark hair. The biggest and the heaviest of the young boxers, he was squeezed into a red T-shirt with the name of the boxing school on it.

Yes, Danny replied.

Who you fighting?

An Argentinean. He's called Ramos.

Is he any good?

Of course he is.

The boy thought about this. Then he said: I think you're going to win.

Thank you.

One of the other boys said: I think so too.

Now run along home, said Ron. Tell your dads you have to pay by the end of next month. And your mums.

The boy with the short dark hair held his fist out to Danny and Danny bumped it with his own. The others copied him.

They trained for about another half hour after that. When the bell went for the last time, Ron pushed the button on the timer, fetched a bottle of water from his bag, had a drink and passed the bottle to Danny.

I'm done in, he said.

Danny poured the water into his mouth through the sports cap. He held his hand under his chin to catch the water that missed his mouth and then splashed it over his face.

What do you think?

Nothing. Too shagged to think, said Ron.

They went out into the corridor. As they reached the changing room, the outside door opened and someone pushed a bike inside. The handlebars got stuck on the door handle and it took a while to free it. It was Ragna. Ron went and held the door open for her. She leant her bike against the wall.

Already finished?

We're going to carry on in a bit, when the others get here.

Okay, she said. I was just passing.

We don't usually let anyone watch, said Ron. He went off to the toilet. She pointed at her bike and said to Danny: My lock's broken.

Danny could feel the cold from outside. He looked at Ragna. She was wearing dark red lipstick.

Did it go well? The training?

Yes, he said.

Her mouth changed and so did her expression. It felt like ages before she said: I'll come in the afternoon next time.

She fetched her bike. Danny held the door open and she disappeared outside. He waited until he could no longer hear her footsteps and then let the door close with a bang.

Isn't she staying? Ron said when he came back.

Not if you're going to talk to her like that.

Like what?

Yeah, said Danny. Like what?

They drank water and when the other boxers got there they trained with them for a while. After the session, Danny pulled off his T-shirt, took his towel out of his bag and went to the showers. He turned on the taps. He took off his underpants, hung them on a heating pipe, gave the cold tap another twist and stood under the shower. The water was hot. He washed his hair. Then he held his face beneath the pulsating stream, closed his eyes and put his hands over his face.

As he was drying himself, he heard Ron talking to someone. He went back into the changing room and found Ron dressed and sitting on the bench with Aaron. The two men fell silent when they saw him.

Don't let me disturb you, Danny said.

Neither of them replied.

Danny got dressed and they headed outside together. Aaron cycled off and Danny walked with Ron to the tram stop. They waited in the shelter.

You really want to win this fight, don't you, mate?

Yeah.

The tram was approaching in the distance. Ron switched his bag over and shook Danny's hand. See you tomorrow.

Yeah, tomorrow.

I'll be on time.

Danny smiled. I'll hold you to that.

Ron turned away.

What was all that about just now? said Danny. That little chat with Aaron?

Nothing.

Ron stood there in silence, just looking down the tramline. You see the way she was looking at you?

What about it?

That's the way women usually look at Sando. Just before they ask if his knob's really as big as they've heard.

Piss off.

Danny turned away. So she works for Varon? he heard Ron say.

Yes.

Since when?

I don't know.

Ron sighed. He tilted his head. Two black guys came and stood beside them. Then they looked at Danny and moved to the next shelter. The tram reached the stop and the doors opened.

She been round before? said Ron. He was standing on the step of the tram, holding onto the pole.

Once.

What a bloody mess.

What do you mean?

Ron looked at him.

What do you mean, man?

Before Ron could answer, the tram doors slid shut.

*

Above the gentle noise of the river comes the occasional crack of a plastic cup, the glug of a bottle, the sound of Robert putting the bottle back on the table and slurping his whisky.

Danny lets Robert pour him a drink. The whisky warms him and makes his thoughts flow smoothly. He says: You sleeping in the car?

There's room for two. Or would you prefer to sleep outside?

I don't know.

It could get cold, says Robert. He hesitates. You're not scared to sleep in the car, are you?

A cold breeze blows across the small of his back. He tugs down the jumper.

I'm not scared.

Or would you rather snuggle up under the sheets with that old biddy?

What old biddy?

The one who was swimming.

No way.

Robert rubs his forehead. Then he blinks at Danny and says: If you want to sleep under a tree somewhere, go right ahead.

Robert stands up and walks over to the car. Danny rests his head on the tabletop and thinks about the bulls. The breeze blows through the grass, accompanied by a quiet humming. Robert repeats the tune three times.

Then he comes back to the table and hands Danny a rolled-up mat. Here, he says, you can sleep on this. I'll go and get you a blanket.

Robert bangs and clatters around in the back of the car and comes back with an old blanket and a torch. He turns on the torch and a powerful beam illuminates the riverbank and part of the river. The water splashes and sparkles in the light.

You could use that to catch rabbits, he says, putting the torch on the table. The wood lights up. Something for that pheasant shooter, he adds.

He turns off the torch. Got everything you need?

I'll be fine.

Danny puts down the blanket on the bench beside him.

I'll leave the door open, Robert says, walking back to the car.

Danny wraps the blanket around his shoulders. He rests his elbows on the table, clasps his hands together. His legs are cold and stiff. He wants to take off his shoes and lie down on the bench, but the cold stops him. He drags his shoes through the sand under the table. A thought goes through his mind: Not far now. Just a short drive and it's time for the bulls.

He stands up, the blanket slips from his shoulders, and he walks down to the riverbank, where the water is quietly gurgling. He holds his fists up in front of his chest. He puffs as he makes a series of jabs, left, left, right hook. He steps through the grass and jabs again, left, left, right hook. Slowly, the cold drains from his body and his blood starts to pump.

He starts walking. He stamps on any thoughts that try to free themselves, crushes them among the pebbles on the riverbank. He climbs up the bridge for the second time. The line of foam on the bank stands out against the sand. By the weak light of the stars, he sees small ripples moving over the water. He breathes out, empties his lungs and starts running, first at half speed, then faster. He runs along the verge, around the bend, through long grass wet with dew.

Panting, he reaches the rock, a solid patch of darkness, the size of the heaviest training balls at the boxing school. He kneels down, wraps his forearms around the cold rock, grits his teeth, tenses the muscles in his thighs and back, and slowly lifts it. He rests it on his thighs. His feet seek a grip in the shingle. He breathes in deeply, breathes out and rolls the rock up to his chest, puts both hands beneath it. Again, he pauses for a moment. Arms trembling, he heaves the rock into the air, its sandy surface rasping his face. With a supreme effort, he straightens his arms. And suddenly he's standing there on the riverbank with an enormous rock above his head. He waits until one of the lights on the campsite goes out. Then he drops the rock onto the shingle, collapses beside it, rolls over the pebbles onto his back and looks up at the stars. The fine sand that was stuck to the rock feels gritty between his fingers.

Back at the table, he unscrews the nearest bottle and takes a swig. He sits down, one hand around the bottle, the other to his ear. He hears a voice. Danny, it says. Her voice.

Something rustles in the grass beside the car. Two rabbits hop through the darkness, stop, sit for a moment, hop some more. They're scrawny little things. His eyes slowly become accustomed to the darkness, and the animals stand out more clearly against the black grass. He spots a few baby ones sitting right by the car. He picks up the torch, intending to pin them down with the beam, but changes his mind, and runs at the creatures. They shoot off in every direction. He stands on the spot where they were sitting.

Her voice again. Counter boxer, she says. She strokes his upper arm. He tenses his muscles and a feeling of euphoria climbs up his neck to his head, a soft, warm tingle on the surface of his skin, but only very briefly, because the wind's picking up and, as he looks over at the deserted river, the warm feeling disappears. He goes back to the bench. He takes another swig, leans back and thinks about the endless horizon of the motorway. Nearly there. He wraps the blanket around his shoulders and lies down on the bench. Cold seeps into him from the ground below. His heart thuds, slow and heavy. His mouth is dry. He runs his hand over his lips. Grains of sand cling to his cheek.

*

Pavel said goodbye and pulled on his coat. I've got to go into town, he said.

See you tomorrow.

Monday.

Monday then.

Pavel opened the door, winked at him and disappeared.

Danny sat on the bench for a while. He drank water from the bottle. Get moving, he said to himself. He took off his T-shirt, pulled his towel from his bag and stood up. He heard a noise out in the corridor. He stayed where he was. The tap of metal on metal. The outside door closed and someone knocked on the door of the changing room.

Anyone in there?

Yeah.

She opened the door and looked into the changing room, first at the bench opposite, then at him. At his chest. She came through the doorway and stopped, holding the door with one hand.

Where are the others?

They're not coming in until this evening.

She nodded. That include the grumpy one?

Yes, he replied.

She came into the changing room, shut the door and leant against it.

I've got to take a shower, he said.

She didn't react, just looked at him.

I've heard you're training hard.

I'm doing my best.

That you're training harder than certain other people.

That's their lookout.

She laughed. Exactly, she said.

Danny slid forward over the bench. The planks felt hard and cold. He had to force himself not to look at her. He looked at his shoes, at the laces snaking across the tiles.

I heard you're going up against an Argentinean.

Yes.

And you're going to give him a pounding.

Who said that?

Someone who knows what they're talking about.

She came closer, sat down on the bench and crossed her legs. She opened her bag, took out a packet of cigarettes and a lighter, pulled out a cigarette and lit it. Danny looked at the cigarette. The filter was red with lipstick.

They say you're a counter boxer.

Danny leant against the wall and then bounced back and rested his elbows on his knees.

Yes, that's what they say.

Is it true?

Depends on the opponent.

Didn't look like it when you were fighting that Bulgarian.

But he was waiting too. So I attacked.

What happens when your opponent goes on the attack?

Then I counter.

Ragna took a drag of her cigarette and dropped it on the tiled floor. The cigarette wasn't even half finished. She crushed it under her heel. Sliding across the bench towards him, she brushed his biceps with her fingertips.

Counter, she said, looking at him. She glanced down and then looked up again, into his eyes, with a different expression on her face. A shock ran up Danny's arm. She withdrew her hand for a moment, and then rested it on his upper arm again before moving it and gently stroking his chest.

I need to take a shower.

Go ahead.

Danny gave her a grin. Then he stood up in front of her and tensed his stomach muscles. She looked at his abs, then up at his face. Still looking him in the eyes, she got up and came closer. And closer still. She kissed him on the mouth. Danny tried to keep looking into her eyes, but she'd closed them. He put his arm around her and she swiftly moved his hand down.

Well, she said.

Her buttocks were small and round and they felt smooth through her trousers. She kissed him wildly. For just one moment, her lips left his and she looked him right in the eye and gave him a smile that seemed full of meaning. He wanted to say something. That she didn't waste any time. Or that she knew what she wanted. But all he could do was smile back at her, watch his gaze reflect in her eyes and repeat what she had said.

Well, well.

She kissed him again, stroked his back and hips, pulled down his shorts, slid her hand into his underpants and took hold of his cock. He squeezed her buttocks, picked her up, turned her around and pressed her shoulders against the wall. Then she was standing above him on the bench. He pushed up her top, tugged her bra over her beautiful little breasts with his teeth and kissed them, licked her nipples. She undid her trousers and let them fall to the floor. He pressed his face into her stomach and listened for a moment to the beating of her heart or maybe his own. She dropped down from the bench, turned him around, pushed him down and sat on his lap. Her hand guided his cock. She slid onto it. She made him keep his legs still while she did all the moving. She kept her eyes shut, held her face to his chest, then higher, over his shoulder, until her forehead was resting on the wall and they were moving together, moving faster. She breathed in his ear until he came, without making a sound.

She sat there for a while. Then she lifted herself off him and turned and sat on his lap, one hand on his chest, his heart.

Counter boxer, she said.

He nodded.

Didn't you want a shower?

Danny nodded and went for his shower. He turned on the tap and let the water flow over his head. Smoke from her cigarette drifted in from the changing room.

*

In the jerky image that's slowly coming into focus, he sees Robert rummaging around in the car.

I'll be off soon, he says.

In the east, on the other side of the river, a narrow strip of blue hangs beneath the black sky. Danny's feet are numb, his arms and legs are stiff, and his body feels as hard and stiff as the bench he's been lying on. The blanket's still around his shoulders, damp and clammy. He stands up, tries to bend his knees. It feels like he has wooden splints strapped to his legs.

I'm not waiting, says Robert.

Danny takes a few steps. Slowly the blood flows back into his feet, into his toes. He can feel them tingling inside his shoes. He hands Robert the blanket and walks around the car. The air is fresh, the grass is wet, the sand is dark with dew. Robert picks up the things from the table and takes them back to the car, where he packs them in amongst the bags. He climbs in and opens the other door for Danny. As Danny's sliding in, Robert starts the engine and presses the button beside the radio. Warm air blows onto his trousers. Danny holds his hands up to the vents, twists the flaps, directing the air flow towards his upper arms. Robert doesn't switch on the radio.

They drive back to the motorway. It's getting lighter as they approach the border and they see a sign for a truckers' stop. Robert says he needs some coffee. And another tasty waitress, if that's not too much to ask. He takes the exit. Three lorries are parked beside the entrance. *Bodega Domeño*, reads a sign above the door. Robert parks in one of the bays. Danny follows him into the café. Robert goes over to a big table by the window, sits down and looks over at the bar and at the door that must lead to the kitchen. Even though there are lorries outside, there's no one else in the café. When Danny's sat down, a man comes out of the kitchen and smiles at them.

Está abierto? Robert asks.

Porqué no?

Un café, por favor, says Robert. *Y podemos comer algo?*

Sí, claro.

Robert orders a large black coffee, an omelette with bread and a glass of orange juice. Same for me, says Danny. The man nods a few times, takes the dishcloth from his shoulder, wipes his hands on it and heads for the kitchen.

Bet he keeps his daughters hidden away in there, says Robert. Looks like we'll have to make do with the old codger.

From where they're sitting, he can see a pointed hill on the other side of the motorway, yellow and parched on top, with scrubby undergrowth around its base. A few small houses lie in the sunlight on the southern slope. The scent of coffee wafts in from the kitchen. Soon the man brings two big bowls of coffee to their table. Robert says: *Gracias*. Danny picks up one of the bowls and sits completely still, staring at the hills. Robert sits opposite him, his head against the wall. He doesn't move either. The man comes out with the orange juice and then brings the omelettes. They watch him as he works. He says: *Aquí tiene y que aproveche*.

When they've finished their breakfast, he comes back and asks them if everything was to their liking. Robert says it was. The man stands there beside their table, as if he's waiting for something.

Vamos a Pamplona, says Robert.

Ya me lo había imaginado.

Para las fiestas, Robert continues. *Para el encierro. Para los toros.*

Está bueno, the man says after a brief silence. He wipes his hands on the dishcloth again. Robert blinks.

What did he say? Danny asks.

Just talking about the bull running. Says it's fantastic.

Don't you speak Spanish? the man says in English. He has a strong accent.

Danny shakes his head.

The bull running is beautiful, says the man. But for people who are not from here it can be dangerous.

Silence.

Robert says: You mean people who aren't prepared.

The man thinks for a moment. Some years ago, an American boy died. The horn of a bull went into his chest and he died on the way to the hospital.

He presses his index and middle fingers into his chest. Then he continues: He fell and did not know that you must stay on the ground. So he got up again.

Robert shakes his head. *Todo el mundo lo sabe*, he says.

Exacto, says the man.

What? Danny looks at Robert.

That American guy got back up, Robert replies. Everyone knows that if you fall over you should stay down.

Yeah yeah, says Danny.

What's the problem?

Nothing.

Have I said something wrong?

You don't need to repeat everything, Danny says quietly.

You asked, didn't you?

I got that bit though, about getting up and staying down.

So why did you ask?

Because I didn't understand all that Spanish crap.

The man smiles at Danny and says in English: Everyone knows, except that American.

Were you there? Danny asks.

Me? No.

The man holds the dishcloth. He beckons to them and, without saying a word, walks over to a corner of the restaurant. Robert looks at Danny. They get up and follow the man. He shows them a framed photograph that's screwed to the wall.

This is Esteban Domeño.

It's a portrait of a man with a dark moustache. He's wearing a black jacket and a hat.

Esteban, the man repeats. He sniffs. They even took his name from him.

What do you mean?

His name. Esteban Domeño. An American wrote a book about the fiesta. He described Esteban's death, but in the book he was called Vicente. They gave him a different surname too. But his real name was Esteban Domeño.

There's fire in the man's eyes. Robert waits for that fire to subside a little before he asks who Esteban Domeño was.

Esteban Domeño was my grandfather. He had a wife and two children. The Americans wrote about his death. God knows why they gave him a different name. They made the fiesta famous all over the world, but our family's name is forgotten. Why is that?

Robert holds his breath.

The man's expression softens. He asks: Why do the Americans come here?

That's a question you'd have to ask them, says Robert.

The man laughs. I already have. They are crazy drunks. And they talk crazy talk about adrenaline. But the fiesta's about more than drinking and smoking that junk and chasing a bit of adrenaline. That's what the Americans made it. The man sighs. But yes, without the

Americans the fiesta would have been forgotten long ago. They write about it, make films, take photographs, print T-shirts. They keep the fiesta alive and at the same time they kill the fiesta. That is what they do, these Americans.

The café owner falls silent, looks at each of them in turn.

Don't do anything crazy, you two.

All they can do is nod.

Go to the bull running, says the man. Do it. Everyone goes to the bull running and they all know the name of Vicente Girones. No one knows the name Domeño. No one knows the Bodega Domeño.

He sighs again. He rolls up the dishcloth and lets it dangle against his thigh. I know how powerful the Americans are. They are so powerful that I am standing here in my own bodega, speaking English.

Danny nods at the photo. How did your grandfather die?

He fell and got back up again.

Him too?

Sí. He knew he was supposed to stay down, but he got up.

Why?

The man shrugs. Only he knows that. And God. He was your age. Can you imagine?

Danny wants to nod, but manages to keep his head still.

He left a wife and two children. A little girl and my father.

Then the man throws the dishcloth over his shoulder. *Más café*?

110

Sí, por favor.

The man disappears into the kitchen. Robert and Danny go back to their table. High above the café, a bird sits on a power line, gently swinging to and fro. The man brings the coffee and the bird flies away. Robert says he'd like to pay. The man takes his banknote, fetches some change, says goodbye to them and returns to the kitchen, flicking his leg with the dishcloth as he goes. They finish their coffee, which tastes a little strange. Then they push the cups away and go back to the car. Robert spots the fly sitting on one of the vents beneath the windscreen. It's not moving. He takes a piece of paper from his seat, puts it on top of the fly and presses down.

*

They walked together to his house. He opened the front door and followed her up the stairs. Two of the four stair lights were broken and he watched her legs as they moved in the semi-darkness. At the last step, he put his hand on her left buttock.

First door on the left, he said.

Even before they were inside, she said: Nice.

He stopped in the doorway and saw that she was looking out of the window in the stairwell, at the dark courtyard below. Her beautiful face was reflected in the glass. He stood behind her and put his hands on her hips. She rested the back of her head on his chest.

Do you know what I thought?

What?

When you came to the boxing school?

No, I don't know.

That you were there for Sando.

She turned around. Sando?

The guy in the photo.

That black bloke?

All of the women who show up at the boxing school are there because of him.

She laughed. Not me, she said, and kissed him.

Come on in, he said.

He led her to his bedroom. She sat on the edge of the bed and slid off her shoes. He turned on the bedside lamp and sat down next to her. Her skin had that same soft copper glow that he'd noticed the first time he'd seen her, not even that long ago.

She lay back. He slid over beside her, leant on his elbow, ran his hand through her hair. She wrapped one arm around his neck and pulled him close. She was less wild this time, but just as focused. Biting her bottom lip, she tugged at his belt. He stood up, took off his clothes. Then he clenched his fists, held them in front of his face. Come on, he said, give me your best shot.

She laughed. Held her small hands in front of her face. Not fists, but rigid, open hands, like an actor in a kung fu movie.

Hiii-yah! she said, flashing her hands through the air.

He shot backwards, ducked, then pounced on her, grabbing hold of her hands and gently biting her neck. She laughed again. She wriggled out from beneath him. He let her go. She kissed his stomach, before moving down to his cock, kissing it long and slow, running her tongue over the tip and then down to his balls, swirling, seeking. He lifted his head and looked down at her dark hair spread over his stomach. Then he slid his arms behind his head and sighed.

She came back up, sat on his thighs and stuck out her tongue.

Hiii-yah! she said again, short and sharp.

Banzai! he shouted back at her.

His strong arms were around her waist. He laid her down on the pillows, with her head hanging over the edge of the bed, and pushed her legs apart. She didn't resist. He lay above her, not actually on her, but hovering over her, supporting himself on his fists and outstretched arms, on his knees. He thrust into her and she twisted beneath him, as though he was attached to her and she couldn't escape. He gazed at her throat with its tensed muscles, her raised chin. He concentrated, listened to her breathing and kept moving until she put her hand on his chest, made him stop for a moment and then pushed down on his backside with her other hand.

Go on, she said. Go on. And he came and he stayed there, hanging above her, for a long time, until the muscles in his arms began to ache. He rolled off her and said: Right, now you can get back to your office.

She thumped him on the shoulder. It was a vicious jab. He grabbed her hips, pulled her across the bed, pushed her hands down into the mattress on either side of her head and said: I want you to come up with a few more of those contracts for me.

She grinned. If you'll sign them.

I'll sign anything.

He let go of her. They lay together on the bed. The beams cast dark shadows on the ceiling panels. He hadn't noticed her take her cigarettes out of her bag or even seen where she'd put her bag, but as he lay there beside her she lit up a cigarette. Her face was illuminated briefly by the flame of the lighter.

So what does your boss think about this?

About what?

You tiring out his boxers.

That's his problem. She thought for a moment. Then she said: Or maybe yours.

4

They race down to the border and cross it without stopping. Robert takes the exit for Pamplona. The sun climbs high above the trees to the left of the road and the land is bathed in a soft yellow glow. The landscape changes, hills become mountains, stones become rocks. The sun climbs slowly, illuminating the sheer walls of rock that they drive past. Small houses and farms cling to the slopes. All he can think about is the bulls. He looks into the cars that they overtake. He sees men dressed in white in some of the cars, with red handkerchiefs around their necks. They wave and gesticulate at Danny. A man blows his horn, pulls up his white T-shirt with one hand and kisses the logo of the football club adorning its front.

It feels like the day of a fight, seeing the other boxers, shaking their hands, having a quick chat – not about boxing, but about the weather, about mutual acquaintances, about nothing in particular.

All going to Pamplona, Robert says with pride. He puts his foot down and the car surges forward. The road heads into the mountains. Black-and-white signs on the bends indicate the direction of the curves.

They pass through a village. The houses are sand-coloured, the roofs red. It's like a scene from a postcard. Mountaintops stand out against the sky in the distance, blunt and green, a cloud hugging one of the summits. The road winds again and they climb higher. More rocks and craggy walls. They follow the white line along the tarmac until they get stuck behind dozens of cars. Robert swears and hits the steering wheel. Four men are sitting in the car in front, squeezed in amongst a pile of bags. They're wearing white shirts too.

Once they're over the mountains, they cross a plateau. Robert takes the opportunity to overtake as many cars as he can. The grass on the verge lies golden yellow in the morning light. The sun was shining through the window on the driver's side before, but it's higher now. It's moved round to the windscreen and is shining in his eyes. Danny takes off the jumper and throws it in the back. Robert pulls down the sunshade and they hurtle towards the ball of fire.

Almost half six, says Robert.

The road rises one last time. When they're over the final hump, he sees a river in the valley below. A cliff rises up on the left bank, and reservoirs lie in the dip on the other side of the road, like big round swimming pools, full of vibrant blue water that gleams against the rocks and the river's twisting course. In the distance, two cathedral towers jut up into the sky.

Cars make their way towards the town centre, pouring into the funnel. When Robert and Danny reach their destination, they find hundreds of vehicles lining the roadside. Robert leans over the steering wheel. It's around here somewhere, he says. Smaller streets climb up along both sides of the road, lined by low buildings, tin sheds, workshops. A garage. A timber yard with huge stacks of wood behind a fence. They drive over two roundabouts. The road's so busy that they have to go at walking pace. The centre's closed to traffic, so Robert parks in a side street. I parked somewhere around here last time too, he says. The road ends in a low fence with the river beneath. He finds a spot beside a tree at the end of the street and parks at an angle to the concrete pavement.

Perfect, Robert says as the engine falls silent. It's not far from here.

The car is practically up against the tree. Danny can't open his door. He has to climb over the gearstick and get out on Robert's side. The sun's down behind the houses, but the air's already warm, even this early in the day. The shutters of the houses are closed.

I'll just grab a few things, says Robert. Then find somewhere to take a leak and we'll be off.

Danny walks over to the water. There's a residential area on the other side of the river. The river curves away on his left. He can see the cathedral beyond the water, stretching high above the rooftops. He wanders back to the car and looks down the street. Men in white shirts are walking down the main road towards the town centre. Robert finishes pissing against the tree. Then he puts a bottle of water in his rucksack, fishes out a red handkerchief from somewhere and drops it into the rucksack. The two men dissolve into the white procession, all heading towards a common goal.

*

117

The bridge over the river runs at an angle to the banks and seems endless. The river curves beneath them and they find themselves walking almost parallel to its course.

Down there, says Robert, nodding in the direction of the old town centre, where the houses huddle together along narrow streets. The crowd shuffles along the pavement as the procession works its way into the town. Once they're over the bridge, they follow a wide road to the left and soon reach the town centre. Robert says: That way. He steers Danny onto the pavement and into a side street where there are fewer people. They walk around a block of houses and down alleyways lined by high buildings with small balconies and metal railings, before coming to a square where the white crowd has gathered. They hear shouting, singing, music. A drum beats incessantly somewhere nearby, while a deeper-sounding drum thuds slowly in the distance. Robert takes Danny by the arm and pulls him past groups of Spaniards and straight through a gang of laughing Americans with glassy, drunken eyes. He can smell the alcohol on their breath. On the other side of the square, Danny sees a sign on the wall: *Plaza del Castillo*. Robert drags him down a narrow alleyway. They reach halfway before finding they can't move backwards or forwards. Bloody gawpers, Robert mutters, pushing people aside. Danny follows him until they bump up against a heavy wooden fence. Through the slats, he can see the long straight street that the bulls are going to run down.

That's the Estafeta, says Robert.

Which direction do the bulls come from?

Robert points. He climbs onto the fence. As Danny puts his hands on the slats, Robert lifts his legs over the top, one at a time, and drops down on the other side.

You can wait here if you like.

Danny climbs over. There are a few men dressed in white on the other side of the street. Otherwise, it's quiet here, compared with the square, but still the air is buzzing with excitement. They sit down on the pavement, their feet in the gutter. White lines are painted on the street in a grid. There's a chemist's shop in the building opposite, with neon letters over the door and people standing on the balconies above.

Robert takes the bottle of water from his bag, unscrews the top and drinks. Wiping his mouth, he hands it to Danny. While he's drinking, Robert takes the red handkerchief out of the bag and ties it around his neck.

If you change your mind, you can always climb back over the fence.

I'm not going to change my mind.

I've only got one handkerchief.

Do you have to wear one?

You don't have to do anything.

The Spaniards are singing their lungs out. The sound echoes around the walls. The monotonous drumming starts up again in the square.

Danny reads the Spanish words on the metal manhole cover beside him and runs his hand over the large, smooth cobbles. He hasn't had a minute to think since they got here. Now that he's sitting on the kerb and the sun's coming up, Ragna's back again. He sees her sitting on the edge of his bed, running a comb through her hair. Sunlight falls through the skylight, making her black hair gleam.

Robert taps Danny on the arm. I'm going that way. You coming?

He's pointing north. They get up. Danny looks left and right. Robert checks his watch. An hour to go, he says. We're still okay to move around.

They head down the street. Men and boys in white shirts are sitting and leaning against the walls. Some nod at them. A man in a T-shirt with a picture on the front yells something at them. Danny doesn't understand what he says. The man comes over and stands in front of him.

I see it in your eyes, he says in heavily accented, drunken English. The picture on his T-shirt is a bull's head. The man says something else about his eyes. Robert comes over and stands between them. Come on, let's go.

Where are you going? asks the man.

That way, Robert says quickly, pulling Danny with him. The man stumbles after them.

Thank you, he says, placing his hand on his heart. Then he disappears.

The long street leads to a wider one, Calle Mercaderes. It's busier there. They can't hear the music from the square now, but there's a group of men kneeling on the cobbles, singing a cappella. They carry on walking and come to another square with a large, ornate building. People are sitting on every step of the building and other spectators are leaning out of the windows of the houses in the next street. A brass band is playing, men in blue uniforms with gold trim on the sleeves. The bull runners fill the streets, holding their red handkerchiefs aloft, the material stretched between their fists. Robert and Danny make their way to the start of the route, down a street called Santo Domingo, which has high walls on both sides.

See those doors?

The street descends to two sturdy metal doors.

That's where the bulls are. Behind the doors.

Most of the people on the street look young, maybe even in their teens. They're singing and shouting and killing time by taking it in turns to run into the street, towards the doors, challenging the bulls. They run back and slap one another on the shoulders, on the back. A little Spanish boy rests his forehead on a man's chest. The man places his hands on both sides of the child's head, kisses it, like a blessing.

Quarter past seven, says Robert.

She's still asleep, thinks Danny. He leans against the wall. He's determined not to think about her. At the same time, he knows that he will think of her, only her, for the next three quarters of an hour, and a few seconds after that.

Robert pushes the bottle of water into his hands. He drinks without thinking. The sun shines on the top of the wall and the line separating light and shade slowly sinks.

Cuarenta minutos, someone calls.

The people on top of the opposite wall are black shadows, moving slowly within a nimbus of soft light. Danny puts his hands to his forehead, warm and damp with sweat, and thinks: It's all a mistake. This entire journey. This town, all this shouting, it's all a mistake.

If you knew I was here, what would you say? Would you come and fetch me? Take hold of me, shake me, force me to climb over that wall? Over that fence? And then we can be together again and you'll put my head on your lap and run your hand through my hair. I'll lie there and hold you tight until you promise to stay with me.

Robert's over by the wall, talking to someone. Danny gets up. He's about to reach out his hand to help her to her feet, as though they're strolling through the town together and he doesn't need to say anything to her, nothing at all.

*

It was March and the nights were freezing, but Danny and Ragna didn't give the sheets time to get cold. He didn't sleep much, didn't really need much sleep. Training was going well. One Saturday morning she asked if he wanted to come into town with her. To the shops.

Fine, he said.

They walked to the luxury shopping street, watched the big, expensive cars driving past, one after the other. Looked in the shop windows, at the clothes, hats, gold jewellery.

I'll buy you a necklace like that one day.

Like that? You're crazy.

As they walked past a café, he heard someone call his name. He recognized Chester, an Irishman who'd trained at the boxing school for a few months, back when Ron and Richard's dad was still around. He was with two other men who Danny didn't know. They were sitting at a table outside, having a beer. Chester stood up and shook his hand.

Long time no see. How's it going?

Yeah, hi. Pretty good, thanks.

Keeping busy?

Yeah.

Chester was watching Ragna out of the corner of his eye. Danny wanted to introduce her, but she'd walked straight past the table, glanced down the road and said: I'm just going to take a look at that place over there. She walked over to the shop next to the café and looked in the window. Danny saw her go into the shop. Chester gestured to him to join them, so he sat down on the empty chair.

Chester introduced him to the other two men, who were visiting from England. He told them Danny was the best boxer in the area and for miles around.

The men looked at him. The smaller one raised his glass and grinned, revealing crooked yellow teeth. He nodded at Danny and took a swig.

Want a drink?

I'm not stopping.

Oh, have a quick one. He pointed at the beers. Or are you on the juice?

I've just had a beer, thanks.

You still training with the Rosenbergers?

Yes. What are you up to?

Oh, you know, this and that, said Chester. He glanced over at the Englishmen. The smaller one had a faded tattoo on his arm.

I know that woman from somewhere.

Probably from those fights in Germany. Gerard Varon.

That's her, is it?

Yes.

Thought so. And you're with her?

Yes.

To keep an eye on her?

What do you mean?

Chester shifted his gaze to the shopping street. Nothing, he mumbled. A big car with dark windows drove past.

Danny asked: You ever worked for Varon?

The occasional thing. An old mate of mine sometimes used to box in Germany and Austria, but that's a while ago now. What about you? You boxing for him?

Yes.

I thought you wanted to give it up.

Decided to carry on for a year or two.

Chester drank some beer and put down his glass. The Englishmen drank too.

You sure you don't want a drink?

I'd better be off.

He waited for her to come out of the shop. She stopped to look in the window again. Then she headed underneath the awning and into the next shop. Danny stood up. He said a cool goodbye to Chester and nodded at the two Englishmen, before pushing his chair back in and walking over to the shop. Ragna was standing by a tall display cabinet of jeans at the back. There was only one pair of jeans on each shelf. She took a pair, unfolded them and held them up for him to see.

What do you think? she asked.

Not bad.

He looked at the door and the big windows. There was no one in sight.

Shall I try them on?

If you like.

No, I don't think so, she said. They left the shop. Outside the café, Chester was talking to one of the Englishmen. The other one had disappeared.

They came to a shoe shop. Ragna looked at the shoes, which were displayed on large white blocks in the window. She pointed at one pair and then they carried on walking. A woman came towards them, with three bags on one arm and a telephone held up to her ear. Danny spotted a coffee house on the next corner in the busy cross street that the trams ran along.

Want to stop for a drink?

She looked at her watch. Just a quick one, she said. They went inside. She ordered an orange juice, he had a water. They sat at a low table next to the window and watched the traffic. Some workmen were digging up the street and the cars had been diverted over the tram tracks. Cyclists wound their way between the cars.

Where do you know him from?

You know, from fights, from before.

She had crossed her legs and was sitting at an angle on her stool. She took a gulp of juice, pulled a cigarette from the packet she'd put on the table and lit it. She spun the wheel of her lighter. It squeaked.

Shopping's more tiring than training.

So why don't you just think of it as part of your training?

She dragged on her cigarette, inhaling deeply, and blew out the smoke. For a long time, they sat in silence. The door opened and a large group of women came in. Four of them sat down by the window. Danny slid into the corner and Ragna moved her stool aside. They were close together now. She stubbed out her cigarette, patted his leg and told him she was popping to the loo. He watched as she inched her way past the women. He downed his water and looked at a tram by the crossing. The driver had got out. He was levering a metal rod between the points of the tram tracks. Danny played with the cigarette packet.

Smoking's bad for you, he heard her say. She sat back down on the stool, her feet tucked behind one of its legs, her knee touching his back. He placed a hand on her back and rubbed his leg against hers beneath the table. Her face was close to his shoulder and for a moment he thought she was going to lean her cheek on it, but she didn't. He looked at her dark eyes. Her long black hair framed her face. Some of her hairs bristled with static and clung to his sleeve.

The women beside them finished their coffee and got up. The sun had moved past the houses now and was shining along the tramline. The rails gleamed.

I have to go, she said.

When am I going to see you?

Tonight.

*

The noise between the walls is swelling by the minute. Danny goes over and joins Robert, who introduces him to the man he's been talking to. They shake hands. He's an Englishman who's been to Pamplona several times before.

How many times have you run with the bulls? he asks Danny.

Never.

A horn drowns out Danny's voice.

Then this is going to be a real experience for you, says the man. Danny leans against the wall, which feels cool. He rests his head against the bricks. Some other Englishmen come and stand with them. Men with tattoos on their arms. A heart with a knife through it. Faded Gothic letters. A man with a big belly and a thick neck who's wearing an England football shirt. He has the logo of a beer company tattooed on his forearm, just above the name of the team he supports. He smiles at Danny and says: Shitting yourself?

No, are you? Danny asks, sitting down.

The man grins.

Ten minutes, comes the call.

As the men continue to dart out and challenge the terrifyingly empty street, Danny sees the man with the bull's-head T-shirt again. He's standing in the middle of the road and he seems to be looking for something. He spots Danny, walks over and sits down beside him. They watch the Englishmen running into the street, in pairs, screaming as they dash back to the group. One man runs so far he can almost touch the door that the bulls are behind. Robert runs out into the emptiness too, together with his English friend. Their armpits are dark with sweat and there's a line of wetness running down Robert's back.

Did you come here with him? asks the man. He tugs at the hem of his T-shirt and the crudely sketched bull's head moves.

I hitched a lift with him.

You didn't know each other?

Not until yesterday, no.

Then he picked the right man.

Danny looks at the man, then down at the ground. The man says: When I saw you, I knew. I thought: he's the one.

You could be right, Danny says quietly.

The man stands up and looks down at Danny. It's something in your eyes, he says. Have you ever looked a bull in the eyes?

No.

You have the same look in your eyes. That's what I wanted to tell you.

He turns around and disappears into the surging white multitude.

The men around him fall silent. Shouts give way to whispers. Then, suddenly, an explosion shatters the tension in the air. A rocket. Like a flash of lightning. Everyone holds their breath for a moment. There's a second bang in the distance, followed by a huge roar, which rings out between the walls. The doors are open, someone shouts. The ground trembles. Danny stands up and positions himself between the high walls. The sound washes towards him like water breaking through a dam. The Spaniards and the Englishmen and the Americans are all shouting. That sound grows louder, almost drowning out the noise of the bulls.

He hears nothing else, as he retreats inside his head, to the hissing and pounding inside his skull, between his temples. In his last thought, he sees Ragna before him. A clear image. Light filtering through the leaves of a plant. Her skin is so pale. She looks into his eyes and he sees something glowing in her dark irises, just for an instant, less than a second. Then her expression changes. Everything changes.

Suddenly he hears a referee counting. Danny sees his white shirt, the cuffs, a glove in the air. A big white thumb that shoots up as the count begins.

One.

His voice barely rises above the noise of the crowd, but Danny can still understand him.

The index finger. Two.

Danny slides his hands into his trouser pockets, puts his feet on the cobbles, closes his eyes and holds his breath. Then he breathes out. He can feel the bulls coming. Six bulls, twelve horns and the sound of twenty-four hoofs stamping on the cobbles. It feels as though his head's inside an oil drum that someone's beating with a stick. Through the pandemonium of Pamplona, the referee carries on counting.

The middle finger. Three.

The hollow sounds change in tone, as though the space has suddenly expanded. A man shouts something.

Ahí vienen los toros. Here come the bulls.

In his head, he is running through Amsterdam again, flying once more through the streets with no idea where to go, just the certainty of leaving everything behind. But right now, in Pamplona, it feels as though his boxing boots are stuck to the cobbles. He thinks about the fight and about her. He knows running isn't an option because the referee's four fingers are held high and his voice is counting, strong and clear. Danny stands his ground. A boxer does not run away, a boxer listens to the count, whether he's the boxer who's been hit and is trying to get to his feet or the boxer who dealt the last blow and is looking down at the opponent lying before him. Both boxers listen to the count.

The glove shakes, all of the fingers are outspread.

Five.

People run past him. They touch his arms. An elbow brushes against his hip. The excited shrieks don't reach his ears. Only Ragna's soft breathing gets through.

The other hand.

Six.

A young Spaniard runs towards him at full tilt. Danny stands there like a rock. The Spanish man tumbles to the ground. Someone helps him to his feet. Danny doesn't budge, just presses his hands to his thighs. Through slitted eyes, he sees the bulls appear, a line of black backs parting the crowd. The boys and men in white are running, fleeing from the bulls. Robert is nowhere to be seen. Danny breathes in, closes his eyes for the last time.

Seven.

The referee's voice is deeper now.

He puffs the dry air out through his nose, as the muscles in his chest tense and he waits for the blow.

Eight.

Something presses into his hip. It's surprisingly gentle. His eyes shoot open and he sees a huge brown bull heading for him. It's not there yet. For a moment, this still life remains intact. The sounds of Pamplona fade away and the bull stands before him, as if frozen. One of its horns juts up into the air, the other is pointing in his direction. The bull's eyes are small black bullets on either side of its head, as dark as its nostrils, which seem so much larger in comparison. In the middle of its forehead is a crest of brown curls. The head is followed by a huge mass of muscles, propelling the bull forward. Again that pressure against his body, as though a hand is touching him, moving down to his stomach, tender yet firm. That hand belongs to her and it strokes gently over his midriff and down his side, just like the first time. He hears the bull snort. Ragna is there in front of him, breathing, planning to launch her attack, but delaying the moment and keeping her distance, first exploring his skin with her fingertips. Darting closer, kissing him. Stepping back, gently blowing on his chest and moving upwards, like the breath he can feel on his neck right now.

The other sounds return. Everything around him starts moving again. As the bull reaches him, two arms grab him around the waist and pull him to the cobbles. The man who tackled him is tossed aside and the noise of the hoofs slips away too, changes pitch, like the sound of a passing car, leaving silence in its wake.

Danny's head is on a smooth cobblestone in the shade. It feels cool on his skin. He watches the bulls thunder past. He sees Robert lying down the street, against the wall. There's no one else in sight. The street seems to have been swept clean. The red handkerchief hangs over Robert's shoulder, the rucksack is by his arm. His lower leg is at a strange angle to his knee.

His trousers are torn and there's a patch of blood on them.

Danny breathes calmly. He slowly turns onto his back and looks up at the blue sky. People come running. He feels one hand on his shoulder and another under his armpit. He is surrounded by shouts in Spanish and English as people help him to his feet.

You okay? an English voice asks.

Yes, yes, he says.

He makes it clear that he doesn't need any help and stands up, but he feels dizzy, so he squats back down and rests one hand against the wall. The circle of people around Robert is growing larger. He walks over, asks them first to let him past, but then has to push his way through. He stops a couple of feet away from Robert. Their eyes meet. Robert just says: Why?

Danny can barely hear him in the tumult of people. The question hovers in the air like a slight vibration, but Danny understands and hangs his head.

Two men in orange jackets appear. One of them is carrying a case with a red cross on it. He puts it down on the pavement beside Robert. People stand aside to make room for them. The men look at Robert's leg. The shorter of the two, a man with a beard, places one hand on Robert's thigh and moves his foot slowly backwards and forwards with his other hand. Robert screams with pain.

Las manos quietas! he barks. There's a brief discussion between the two men. Robert groans and swears. Someone shouts into a walkie-talkie. Robert uses that dead time to look at Danny and repeat: Why?

Danny doesn't answer.

Why did you just stand there?

The blood trickles out of his trouser leg, forming a dark red puddle on the cobbles and seeping into the gaps between the stones. Danny looks away.

*

She stepped out of her clothes, left her trousers lying on the floor, dropped her shirt on top of them. She had two birthmarks on her hip. It felt as though he was seeing them for the first time, as though they had been applied to her skin since he last saw her. She held out her hand, came closer, kissed him gently on the mouth and led him to the bed. He pushed the sheet aside, knelt on the edge of the bed and waited for her to lie down, slim and naked and beautiful.

Come here, she said.

He stayed where he was, looking at her.

Come here.

He slid over to her and pulled up the sheet. He heard the siren of an ambulance going down the road. The sound ebbed away. She lifted her head, he put his arm under it, and she turned her face to kiss his shoulder, his chest. It was very quiet in the room. His body was rigid.

Danny, she said softly.

Her eyes were wide. He felt her leg rubbing against his. She turned onto her side, kissed him with closed eyes, nuzzled her forehead into his neck, climbed on top of him. She raised her bottom in the air. His cock felt big. It throbbed in her hand, then inside her. He could feel her heart thumping against his skin. His own heart thudded to the same rhythm, but at the same time it seemed to have stopped: his blood stood still in his veins and his thoughts were frozen. In that ice, a phrase was carved: To keep an eye on her.

*

The men from the Red Cross try to get Robert onto a stretcher. They tug at his arms. One of them takes hold of his shirt with two hands and pulls him up by his waist. All that time, Robert is looking at Danny. When he's finally lying on the stretcher, the man with the bull's head on his T-shirt appears for the third time. He says: I knew you were the one this year.

The man thumps his chest with his fist, holds it over his heart. Then he goes over to the stretcher, kneels beside Robert, bends over him and whispers something in his ear. One of the men from the Red Cross places a hand on the man's shoulder. He slowly stands up and walks away. Danny follows the man, stops him.

What did you say to him?

The man strokes his mouth with his thumb and says: That I underestimated him.

What else?

That was all.

The man taps two fingers on the side of his head in farewell. Another explosion fills the air.

The bulls are in the arena, says the man.

A rocket bursts, faint against the blue sky.

It's over, he says.

Danny sees his face change, but the same dark power still emanates from the head of the bull on his T-shirt.

He points at Danny's chest, says goodbye and walks away.

The men have taken Robert to the ambulance. They're closing the doors. Danny starts to head down the street without knowing where he's going. The little man from the Red Cross steps out in front of him. Handing him Robert's rucksack, he asks in English: Did you come here together?

Danny nods.

Are you coming to the hospital with him?

Me?

Who else?

It sounds like the logical thing to do. The expression on the man's face and the reflection of the sunlight on his orange jacket rob Danny of any reply. He follows the man to the ambulance. Robert is lying on a narrow bed, fastened in with thick straps. He's staring at the ceiling. Danny waits outside for a moment. The little man places a hand on his back and signals at him to get in. He ducks as he climbs inside. Then he puts the rucksack on the floor and sits on a fold-down seat beside Robert. They drive off. The ambulance swings around a few bends and stabilizes before accelerating.

Robert rests his hands on his stomach and laces his fingers together. You didn't have to come, he says. His voice seems a long way off. His head rocks from side to side and his gaze is distant.

He looks down at his limp leg. Danny follows his gaze. His jeans have been cut open and the denim is dark red, almost purple in places.

After a while, the ambulance slows down and goes over a bump. They come to a stop, the doors open and someone appears with a wheeled stretcher. The ambulance men aren't exactly gentle when they slide Robert onto the trolley. He screams and swears as they move him. A black man in a white coat pushes him inside. Robert tells him to take it slowly, but the man pays no attention.

Danny follows them. As he passes through the sliding doors and into the lobby, he feels the cool air on his neck. He hears someone crying. It's an old Spanish woman in a black headscarf sitting on a bench in the corridor. She's wailing and her sobs seep into the lobby, constant, unremitting, like a dripping tap.

The man pushes Robert into a room in the emergency ward. It's a small room, square and white, with a curtain around it. The man parks the trolley by the wall and leaves. Danny sits down on a chair and waits. Neither of them says anything. After a while, a doctor appears from behind the curtain. *Buenos días*, he says. He takes a quick look at Robert's leg and turns to Danny.

What happened? the doctor asks in English.

You'd better ask him that.

The man turns to Robert, repeats his question.

I speak Spanish, says Robert.

The doctor turns back to Danny. Did he fall? In the bull running?

Danny nods. He leans back against the cold washbasin. The doctor examines Robert's leg and the wound on his thigh. He asks if he can move his leg, if he can move his foot. Then the doctor uses hand gestures and broken English to explain that they're going to do some X-rays to see if they can set the bone or if they'll have to operate. The doctor turns back to Danny.

Can you fill in the paperwork for him?

Yes.

The doctor goes away. A little later, a man with a clipboard pushes the curtain aside. He hands the clipboard to Danny, who looks at the form that's attached to it. He doesn't know Robert's address or even his surname, but he says: I'll fill it in.

Just put it down, Robert says as soon as the man's disappeared through the curtain. I'll do it later.

Two nurses come and push Robert away somewhere. Danny stays behind. There's a mirror above the washbasin, a small rectangular one. Now and then, he glances up at the polished glass and the reflection of the curtain. It's a long time before they bring Robert back to the room. His leg is straight now. The men push the bed to the wall, put the brake on and leave.

What are they going to do?

Plaster.

Is it broken?

Yes, when I fell. A clean break, they said.

What about the wound?

They're going to bandage it up.

Danny thinks of the car and the photo on the dashboard. The curtain flutters occasionally, but no one comes into the room. Robert wants to sit up, but his leg's too painful. He swears. Danny helps him up.

Could you get me a glass of water?

He nods at the washbasin, which has a glass on it.

Danny fills the glass from the tap, without looking in the mirror. Robert takes a couple of sips. After a long silence, he says: Why did you just stand there?

Why did you come back?

Danny turns his face to the curtain. Halogen lights are glowing in the corridor behind it, casting patches of light on the material and making it glow bright green.

He walks through the curtains and sits down on the bench in the corridor. The old woman's no longer there. Two large men are pushing a trolley with an unshaven man on it, who's bleeding from a head wound. A boy, just a child, is walking beside the trolley. He's talking to the man in Spanish. As they pass the bench, Danny smells the sharp odour of wine. The boy has a brown stain on the seat of his trousers.

*

He gritted his teeth and pounded the punch bag, which swung on its chains. Left, left, right hook. His gloves thudded against the blue leather.

You don't have to go all out, said Ron.

Danny jabbed again. Left, left, right hook, in rapid succession. His gloves flashed. He was sweating. He jabbed again and kept on jabbing until the bell went and he sat down a short distance away from the punch bag, his eyes still focused on the leather.

I'll just keep my mouth shut then, said Ron.

He'd arranged to meet her after the training session at a café close to the boxing school. Danny's hair was still damp from the shower. He had an orange juice and Ragna drank red wine. She smoked a cigarette and asked him how it had gone that evening.

Well, he said.

Did you leave the other guy in one piece?

Yeah.

Are you on schedule?

He nodded.

How long is it now? About six weeks, right?

Seven.

He had nothing else to say to her. He emptied his glass. After a while, he said: I'm tired.

They stood up and walked out together.

If it's okay with you, he said, I'm going home. To sleep.

Have a rest, she replied. You need it.

She kissed him and they walked together to her bike. She undid the lock, clicked it back together, hung it over her handlebars and turned the bike around. Then she swore. What's wrong? he asked.

Puncture.

She looked at the back wheel. He pressed the tyre to the rim with his thumb.

Want me to go in and see if they've got a pump?

Yeah, please.

He took a look at the wheel. No point, he said. The valve's gone.

I'll just have to walk.

Want me to go with you? I can come back for my bike later, Danny said.

Thought you were tired.

I'll manage.

Just go home and sleep, she said, and kissed him again. She turned the bike and pushed it down the pavement past the café. Danny headed in the other direction. When he reached the corner, he stopped and turned around. He could see her in the distance, walking past the park, going round the corner. He retraced his steps. At the corner, he stopped to watch her again. She was walking down the side of the park, past the houses. Danny followed her at a distance, walking down the narrow pavement beneath the trees. She went down the street until she reached the water, where she cut through behind the parked cars, crossed the canal, tugged her bike up onto the opposite pavement, and then headed down the other side of the water towards the petrol station. From there, she followed the wide road with the tramline. Danny went after her, but kept his distance. He had an idea where she might be heading. His heart was thumping, but it wasn't from walking.

She took a side street that led to another canal and stopped at the fourth lamppost. She leant her bike against the lamppost, locked it up and disappeared into the porch.

He stopped opposite the house, by the water, hidden behind a van. He stood beneath a huge ash tree. He saw the light on the first floor go on. Then it went out and the light on the second floor came on and someone closed the curtains.

Working? he muttered. Like hell.

He walked back along the dark canal. He took the valve out of his trouser pocket and threw it into the water.

*

The air in the hospital corridor seems perfectly still. The doctor who took the X-rays comes over to the bench where Danny's sitting and asks, in perfect

English: Would you please be so kind as to inform his family?

Danny shrugs.

He can't do it himself. He has to go to the plaster room.

But I don't know his family.

The doctor glances down the empty corridor. Then he looks back at Danny and shrugs. Okay, I'll do it, Danny says.

The doctor hands him the clipboard. You can phone from there, he says, pointing at a counter along the corridor before hurrying away. Robert has already filled in his name, address and telephone number. With the code for the Netherlands in front. Danny goes over to the counter. The receptionist looks up at him and he sees that she has thick, dark eyebrows. He asks if he can use the phone. She points at it and goes back to shuffling her papers. Danny dials the number. The phone rings a few times.

Hello. The hesitant voice of a young boy.

Could I speak to your mum?

Who is it?

My name's Danny. I'd like to speak to your mum.

Who is it? The little boy's voice grows faint. A clicking sound echoes down the line and then he hears another voice: Hello, this is Manuela. Sorry about that.

Yeah, hello, says Danny. I'm calling about your husband.

The girl at the counter looks up. Danny turns away.

And you are?

Danny. I hitched a lift with him.

Oh yes, he mentioned you, she says. Her tone is cool, but her breathing has become more rapid. Then she pulls herself together.

What's happened?

He's broken his leg.

She gasps. Broken?

He can hear both fear and relief in her voice. Danny lets the relief sink in, ignores the fear, and says: They're putting it in plaster.

So what happens now?

He can hear the children playing in the background, the high-pitched voice of a little girl: Daddy, Daddy. Just a moment, says Manuela. She tells the children to be quiet. So what happens now? she asks again. Will he have to stay there?

I don't know.

When will you find out?

Probably later today, says Danny.

She hesitates, then says: Could you call again when you know? Tell me what's happening?

Danny doesn't reply.

Will you do that?

Yes, he replies quietly. They say goodbye. He hangs up and thanks the receptionist with the dark eyebrows. She smiles. He walks back down the corridor. Robert's lying on the bed, waiting.

Did you call her?

Yes. She asked what had happened.

What did you say?

That you've broken your leg.

Anything else?

She asked when you'll be back.

Didn't you tell her anything else?

No.

They are silent. A man appears and signals that he has to take Robert with him. He takes the brake off and pushes the bed out of the room.

*

Danny goes through the sliding doors, out into the bright sunlight, and shades his eyes with his hand. The hospital is in a residential district. No sign of the cathedral. He walks around the building. There's a car park to the west of the hospital, with an industrial estate beyond. Danny walks down the path, between large potted plants whose leaves hang dry and limp on clay pellets. He goes around two corners and sees the town centre. When he finds a nice spot in the shade, he stops and gazes out over the red roofs and cathedral towers.

The sun moves on and the light falls on his face, warming his cheeks. He squeezes his eyes shut and sits for a long time, leaning against the wall. Over an hour later, he heads back inside, but the curtained room is empty and there's no one around who might be able to tell him something. He goes back outside, sits in the same spot and waits. All that time, he thinks about his conversation with Robert's wife. The concern in her voice. The children screaming in the background. He thinks about Robert and about the car. He knows what he has to do.

A man comes shuffling down the path.

Estás bien?

143

Sorry? Danny says, standing up.

Everything okay? the man asks in English. His voice sounds hoarse.

Fine.

And your friend?

He's going to be okay.

Has he gone to the – what do you call it? – for the plaster.

Yes.

The man's wearing an open dressing gown. His body is pale and thin. An old, hairless chest. Danny only notices now that he's holding onto a rickety-looking drip stand. The man says: I saw you come in. I saw his leg. Is it broken?

Yes.

The man moves closer. The wheels of the drip stand squeak along the pavement. He stops beside Danny in the narrow strip of shade and says: The doctor told me I only had another four weeks to live.

Danny breathes out through his nose. He says: Four weeks?

Sí, says the man. That was six years ago.

He's holding onto the stand as though he needs the support. Maybe he wants to show Danny how shaky it is or how shaky he is himself. Then the man says: Your friend's leg is going to be fine.

The man looks up at the sky. Danny does the same.

Six years, the man repeats. I wanted to go to La Palma. With my children and grandchildren. For Christmas. Well, I've been there the past five years and I'm going again in December. I've already booked the house.

Danny looks down. He places his hand on his chest and feels his heart beating. He looks at the thin old man. The man coughs.

The doctor didn't know I wanted to go to La Palma.

You went with your children?

And my seven grandchildren.

Danny hesitates. What if your situation had been different?

What do you mean?

What if you hadn't had any children?

But I do have children.

But what if you didn't? Can you imagine what that would be like?

The man purses his lips. It's hard for me to imagine, he says. I suppose the doctor might just have been right then.

They both look down at the town. The air above the buildings ripples in the sun.

I'm going back inside.

Tell your friend he's going to be fine.

I will.

Danny steps away from the wall. The man turns to follow. One of the wheels gets caught in the paving slabs and the stand judders and then comes free. They say goodbye. Danny heads inside. Robert is waiting in a wheelchair in the curtained room. His leg is in plaster up to the knee, and his ruined jeans are fastened around it with safety pins. Six weeks, he says.

Six weeks.

I've got to wait for the doctor, says Robert.

Danny sits down and they wait in silence for the doctor. When he comes, he tells them they're free to go.

They shake his hand and say goodbye and the doctor disappears again through the curtains.

Could you push me outside?

*

The doorbell echoed down the corridor, three times in quick succession. Then a short silence, followed by another ring, a long one this time. He stayed where he was, sitting on the edge of his bed. He swallowed. Another ring, louder and longer than before. He picked up his jogging bottoms from the floor and was about to put them on, but changed his mind. He waited. The phone rang. He stared at it as it rang four times before switching to the answering machine. He listened to his own voice and to the beep.

It's me, I'm at the door.

Silence, rustling, a car driving past.

Are you in? Please pick up. Danny. She sighed. Danny, came the voice again through the speaker.

He walked over to the phone, picked up the receiver and turned off the answering machine. He didn't say anything.

Are you there?

Yes.

Could you open the door?

He was silent.

Danny, open the door.

Are you on your own?

Yes, she said firmly.

He pulled on his jogging bottoms, gave his T-shirt a sniff, tucked it in, fastened the drawstring of his jogging bottoms and slid his feet into his trainers. Without doing up the laces, he headed down the four flights of stairs. She was standing in the porch, her hands on the frosted glass, her face between them, peering in. He turned the key and opened the door. Ragna stepped back.

Can I come in?

He looked around, rubbed his temples: So you didn't bring him with you?

Who?

You know very well.

Just let me come in for a moment.

He looked at her.

What were you doing over at his place?

I work for him.

That late? With the lights off? Right.

He started to close the door.

Wait.

Her hand was on the doorframe. Danny held onto the door.

I can explain.

He opened the door a little wider, looked into her eyes and saw what he wanted to see. He held the door open for her. Ragna followed him upstairs in silence. When they reached his flat, she stopped just inside the door.

I heard you're not training.

He said: What difference does it make? His voice was harsh.

She looked at the table, at the chairs. Sat down. Putting both hands on the table, she slowly said: I can explain about Mr Varon.

What's with the 'Mr'?

A brief silence.

He brought me here.

Danny stopped in the middle of the room and listened.

She said: He's like a father to me.

He brought you here?

Yes.

Where did you meet him?

In Thailand, at a boxing gala.

She told him that she had been born in northern Thailand, but ended up in Bangkok when she was still very young. She'd met Gerard Varon at the fights in Pattaya. The next time he was there he asked her to come back to the Netherlands with him.

And you went with him? Just like that?

After some ... negotiation.

Negotiation? With your family, you mean?

She thought for a moment. With the people who looked after me.

Your foster family?

You could call them that, she said. I left for the Netherlands. Wheeled him onto the plane and off again. I learned the language. I learned about the people.

She paused for a moment.

Life's good here, she said. In spite of the cold.

Why did he take you with him?

He didn't want to abandon me.

And it was that simple?

She nodded.

I thought there was something going on between the two of you.

Ragna spread out her hands on the tabletop and then brought them back together. She shook her head as she looked at him. You know he's paralyzed from the waist down? she said.

So?

She held her hand level with her navel and said: Nothing works beneath this point.

Danny put his hands in his pockets. He went and stood beside her. Everything was clear.

You'd better start training again.

Is that what you came to tell me?

That's my job.

Ragna got up and went over to him. She raised one hand to his neck and stroked his stubble.

Sorry I didn't tell you sooner.

Her eyes told him she meant it.

Doesn't matter.

She reached for her cigarettes. She took one from the packet and lit it. He fetched an ashtray from the kitchen and put it on the table. Watched as she took a drag.

Sorry, she repeated. Her voice was quiet.

Later that evening, he ordered two pizzas and they ate together at the table. He asked her about Thailand and her foster family. She said: I'd like to go back, but not for good.

He nodded.

She asked him where he came from.

I've travelled around a lot.

Far?

No. We were with the fair. We never went very far, just Holland and Belgium, but we were in a different place every week.

Do you still see your family?

Not often. My parents live quite close, but I don't visit them much.

When they'd finished eating, Ragna asked if she could stay.

He said she could.

They made love. She fell asleep in his arms. He looked up at the beams, ran his hand over his legs, his stomach, his cock. He felt big and strong, but at the same time a feeling of lightness rose up within him, a feeling like the shiver during a fight when he'd landed that final jab and his muscles were about to relax and he'd look at his opponent and hold on to the tension in his body until it was all over. But now, in his attic room, that feeling lasted much longer.

*

Danny hoists Robert's rucksack onto his back and pushes the wheelchair into the corridor and out of the building, across the car park in front of the hospital. He holds on tight to the handles. The wheelchair rolls easily, as though it's empty, but the rubber handles feel heavy in his hands. He grips so hard that his forearms hurt.

They go over a hump and he holds back the wheelchair as they roll down the other side.

That way, says Robert.

Danny doesn't respond.

It's that way.

Just going down the kerb.

He pushes the wheelchair between two parked cars and onto the road, crosses over, and bumps it back up onto the pavement. The sun is behind him, burning his shoulders. He closes his eyes for a moment.

The road goes uphill and around a corner. When they reach the top of the hill, Danny stops and looks at the downhill slope, with its parked cars, lampposts along both sides, a few rubbish bins, a letterbox. A wall painted yellow. He lets go of the handles. The wheelchair stays where it is.

*

Following Robert's directions, he goes down a large road to a roundabout, takes one of the exits and comes to the bridge. Danny sees the town lying to their right in the blazing sun. Once they're on the other side of the bridge, he recognizes the wide street and little side roads. He pushes the wheelchair around a corner and sees the car standing there, beside the tree. Robert takes the keys out of his pocket and asks Danny to open the door and help him into the car.

You can't drive with that leg.

Just help me.

It's not going to work.

I want to try.

With that leg?

It's in plaster. It'll be fine.

Wouldn't you rather stay in a hotel?

No.

Danny supports Robert as he hops to the car on his left leg and sits on the edge of the driver's seat. Swearing, he forces his knee under the steering wheel. He puts the key in the ignition and turns it. The engine roars to life. Robert rests his plaster cast on the pedal and tries to put his foot down. He moves his hand to the gearstick and looks down at his leg. Leaning forward, he uses both hands to shift his foot, staring in concentration at the windscreen. He tries again to push the pedal down, but his heel's too bulky and he can't apply any pressure.

Did you really think it was going to work?

Yes.

All the way home?

So what the hell am I supposed to do? He taps his thumb on the wheel.

A cat slinks behind the car, a ginger one with white patches. It moves silently past the wheels, crosses the pavement and walks along the wall. Then it sits on a step in front of a door with a roll-down shutter and licks its paws before continuing on its way. Danny watches as it disappears behind the building by the water.

I can drive, he says.

They look at each other, Robert's eyes small, pensive, blinking; Danny squinting in the sun. Robert leans back, tilts his head.

You don't have to do that.

But I can.

Robert shakes his head. I'd rather go back on the train, he says. He rests his hands on the top of the wheel.

I'll drive, says Danny.

Are you sure?

Do I have to ask a hundred times?

He waits. Robert stares through the windscreen.

Tell you what, says Danny. I'll go over there for a quick piss and when I get back, you can tell me what you want to do.

He walks over to the edge of the water and unzips his jeans. The water ripples gently beneath him. He looks around for the cat, but it's vanished. When he gets back to the car, Robert's still sitting in the driver's seat. Danny leans against the door.

Why did you just stand there? Robert asks quietly.

Danny doesn't answer.

You just going to keep quiet? Like you always do? He runs his hand through his hair. Did you think I'd let you just stand there with those bulls coming?

Yes.

You were wrong.

Danny puts his foot up on the front wheel. I never asked you for anything.

You think I asked for this? Robert places both hands on his thighs, rubs them on his jeans. You're not going to tell me, are you?

Danny pushes the tyre with his foot and the car rocks. No, I'd rather not.

Then you'd better go.

What about you?

I'll think of something.

Danny rests his forearms on his knee. The sole of his shoe squeaks on the tyre. What about the car?

I'll get someone to pick it up.

I'm going to drive you home.

This time he says it in a tone that Robert can't argue with. He just says: Fine. He tries to get out of the car, but he can't manage by himself. Danny helps him into the wheelchair, pushes him around the car and parks him next to the tree. I'll get the car out onto the road first, he says. He walks back around the car, climbs in, starts the engine and manoeuvres the car onto the road. Then he gets out and helps Robert into the passenger seat. Danny folds up the wheelchair, lifts it into the boot, puts the rucksack on the back seat and gets into the driver's seat.

Robert says: Could you get a clean shirt out for me?

Danny takes a T-shirt from one of the plastic bags. He passes it to Robert.

Not that one.

Something wrong with it?

Not a white one. There's another one in there.

Danny finds a green T-shirt at the bottom of the bag. Robert takes off his dirty shirt, tosses it into the back of the car and puts on the clean one. They sit there for a moment, looking at the river, the cathedral and the red roofs. Danny says a silent farewell to Pamplona.

He reaches for the lever under the seat and pushes it back. Then he starts the car and returns to the main road. He takes the turn for the bridge and heads to the hospital, drives into the car park and stops at the main entrance. While Robert waits, he takes the wheelchair from the boot, unfolds it and pushes it through the sliding doors and into the lobby. I'll just leave it here, he says to the receptionist.

Don't you need it? she asks. You're welcome to borrow it.

No, thanks. It's okay.

He drives west along the river. The sun is up high above the hills. The route they followed down to the river that morning winds up the slope on the opposite bank in the blazing sunshine.

*

She was on her elbows, her head on the pillow, her buttocks in the air. With every thrust, she moaned, rhythmically, powerfully. He put his hands on her hips, held her in place, and gave it to her. She pressed her face into the pillow. He watched her dark hair swishing from side to side. He heard her muffled moans rising up from the pillow, slowly becoming a pleading repetition of his name. Danny, Danny, Danny. He tensed the muscles in his abdomen and felt himself drain empty.

Later she said: Know what? You're a real boxer, you are.

How do you recognize a real boxer?

She put her hand on his crotch, squeezed his balls.

He laughed.

She got up, walked over to the chair and took her cigarettes from her trousers. Standing there naked and small in his attic room, she lit a cigarette and looked over at the window. It was getting light in the east. She took a drag on her cigarette and said: Believe me, I know how to recognize a real boxer.

So do you fuck all of your boxers?

She walked around the bed, took another drag on her cigarette. No, not all of them.

Silly cow, he said. He picked up the pillow and threw it at her. She held the cigarette close to her body.

Hey, watch out, she said.

He picked up another pillow, waved it in the air and grinned at her. He said: I'm going to knock that fag clean out of your paws.

Cut it out.

I will if you will.

Ragna smiled. I only fuck real boxers, she said.

Yeah? Well, I'm the only real boxer around here.

Right, Ragna said slowly. I've seen the photos for Leipzig. For the poster. Now those guys look like real boxers.

Who?

The ones from Leipzig.

Was Ramos on the poster?

Yes.

So you think he's a real boxer?

She sat down on the edge of the bed, facing him, and said: Yeah. A very real one.

What do you mean?

You know, just saying.

He grabbed hold of her shoulders and pulled her towards him. Then he pushed her down onto the mattress and nuzzled into her neck, giving it a nip. She yelped. He slipped his hands under her armpits and picked her up. I'll show you a real boxer, he said.

5

They're driving along a three-lane toll road, passing through rolling, ochre-coloured countryside. American music is playing on the radio – Danny's found a different station. He stays in the right-hand lane. Occasionally, other cars overtake them, quickly disappearing into the distance. His hands rest loosely on the bottom of the steering wheel. The sun is on his side of the car. The road turns and the sun turns with it. Now it's shining in his eyes. He pulls down the sunshade. Robert's slumped beside him. His paunch looks bigger, but his tic appears to have calmed down.

Where did you put that bottle of water?

In the bag, I think.

Where's the bag?

Back seat.

Robert turns around and looks over his shoulder at the back seat. Damn it, he says.

Want me to stop?

Stop somewhere later.

She asked me to let her know what's going on.

What did you say?

That I would.

Robert rubs his neck and quietly clears his throat.

You can call her when I stop somewhere, Danny says.

How am I going to get to a phone?

I'll help you.

It'd be easier if you just gave her a quick call.

She's your wife.

You're the one who promised to call.

Robert's sitting at an angle, his leg jammed awkwardly beneath the dashboard.

First let's find somewhere to stop, says Danny.

As they approach a petrol station, Danny points at the sign. Robert says: No, let's stop at the next one.

Thought you were thirsty.

For a long time, the hum of the engine and Robert's heavy breathing are the only sounds inside the car. They roll northwards, kilometre after kilometre. They pass close to a city and go through a cloverleaf interchange, then under several flyovers. Now and then, Robert swears and rubs his thigh. Danny holds on tight to the steering wheel. His thumbs point to the sky. A lorry with a huge double trailer loaded with concrete sewer pipes overtakes them. They can feel the suction as it passes. Danny turns the wheel to compensate.

Do you think she's angry?

I don't know.

Robert stares at the tarmac. He shifts to the middle of the seat, slides one hand under his leg and supports the plaster. A blue Mercedes with a German number plate flies past. When it's just a dot in the distance, Robert says: Well, she's not exactly going to be happy about it, is she?

*

The air in the zoo's nocturnal house was humid. The voices of schoolchildren rang along the dark hallway where the enclosures lay behind low barriers. They stopped at one of the enclosures. He pointed out the crocodile to her. It was a spectacled caiman, lying with its tail in the sand and its body in the water, with its nose up close to the glass. A little one, he said. Ragna put her hand on his back and hooked her finger through one of his belt loops.

Beside him, a group of five boys pushed against the barrier.

Go on, touch it, said one of the boys. The other boys laughed.

I can't reach, another boy replied.

He's too scared.

I'm not. I just can't reach.

One of the other boys looked at Danny. What about you? he said. You could reach.

Do I look like I'm crazy?

But it's asleep.

Yeah, right.

You can see it's asleep.

Ragna pinched him.

Fine, said Danny. More children came over. Danny rolled up his sleeves.

Are you lot certain it's asleep?

Sure.

I'll give it a go then.

He's going to do it, Sam. You've got to see this.

Two girls who'd just joined them squealed with excitement. He's going to do it. He's going to do it!

The boy called Sam said: Told you so. His hair was in cornrows. He had light brown skin and was wearing a baseball shirt. He smiled at Danny and said: I knew you'd do it.

The other boys nodded.

Danny leant over the barrier, a sheet of glass with a metal railing. There was a ridge of Plexiglas around the bottom and warning stickers all over the enclosure showing pictures of a mouth with sharp teeth.

Are you absolutely certain it's asleep?

The boys whooped. One of the boys shouted: Yeah, of course. It's hibernating.

Okay then.

Danny bent forwards, his stomach on the railing, and slowly lowered his arm. The crocodile didn't move. Danny wiggled his fingers. He glanced at Ragna. She prodded him. Go on, she said.

So Danny did. He hesitated as he touched the water. The crocodile seemed to be looking at him. Then he scooped up a handful of water and yelled as he splashed it over the children. They scattered. The girls at the front screamed. A blond boy tripped over one of the pillars that were designed to look like mounds of mud or jungle trees. When the children realized what had happened, they laughed and came back to stand beside Danny.

That was a good one, said Sam.

Yeah, I thought so.

Ragna smiled at him and put her arm back around his waist. They walked past the other dark enclosures to the exit. He bought two drinks at the kiosk outside and the two of them sat down and leant against the

160

glass of the hippopotamus enclosure. The hippo was nowhere to be seen and there was no water in its pen.

Nice kids, said Danny.

Yes.

Especially that mixed-race boy. Danny pinched her leg.

Cut it out, Danny, she said.

You could try sounding a bit more enthusiastic.

What do you mean?

Well, you know. I mentioned the mixed-race kid for a reason.

Ragna took a swallow of her drink and felt the bubbles in her stomach.

*

Danny sees the service station. He points the car at the exit lane and leaves the motorway. He drives around the curves, past the petrol pumps and parks just beyond the building. The radio's silent. He can't see a telephone by the shop. Hang on, he says. He gets out and walks around the back, where he finds a payphone on the wall beneath a little plastic shelter. When he gets back to the car, he says: There's a payphone back there.

Robert points at his leg.

Come on, says Danny. He takes hold of Robert's arm and helps him out of the car. Robert doesn't cooperate. His body feels heavy. Once he's out, he stands beside the car, putting his weight on his good leg. Danny helps him to the telephone. There's a litter bin beside the building. Danny pushes it over to the telephone and Robert sits on the lid.

Got any change?

Yes.

Robert digs some coins out of his pocket. Could you get that bottle first?

Danny fetches the bag from the back seat, walks back to the telephone, takes the bottle out of the bag, unscrews the top and passes it to Robert. He takes a few big gulps.

I'll just go and get some petrol, Danny says when Robert hands back the bottle. He walks back to the car, drives over to one of the pumps and fills it up. Then he parks up and goes over to look at the newspapers in the rack outside the shop. All French. He walks around the back of the building and watches Robert talking on the phone, his eyes half-closed. He heads inside the shop and wanders past the shelves. When he hears Robert calling him, he walks back to the telephone.

Everything okay?

Yes.

What did she say?

Take me back to the car first.

Danny puts his arm around Robert's shoulders. Robert hops to the car. He settles into his seat and Danny hands him the bottle.

Have you paid?

No.

Robert gives him some money. Danny goes inside to pay, comes back, starts the car in silence and drives to the exit.

She was furious, says Robert. Holding his cast with both hands, he slides across the seat. Danny grips the steering wheel really hard. His knuckles are white.

But she's glad I'm coming back.

Danny wants to ask what else she said. But he keeps quiet, cranks up the speed and stays in the left-hand lane for a long time. There are no other cars in the rear-view mirror.

*

The saucer that she used as an ashtray was on the wooden floor beside the bed. He watched the smoke as she blew it out. He stroked her neck and she tipped her head back.

His body was tired from the evening training session. His legs lay leaden on the mattress. Even though his head felt so light, the arm supporting it still tingled. He moved his arm and rested his head on the pillow. If he closed his eyes, he'd be asleep within a couple of seconds. He kept looking at her.

She took one last drag and stubbed out her cigarette. She picked up the lighter from the floor and ran it through her fingers, spun the wheel. He slid one hand under her stomach, which felt soft.

I'm going back to Thailand, she suddenly announced.

Danny didn't say anything.

For a few months.

That long? When?

Soon, she said. I'm going to visit some people.

She took a fresh cigarette from the packet and tapped it on her temple.

Yeah, I'm free to go. I can visit whoever I like.

You are coming back, aren't you?

Of course.

The beams and shadows on the ceiling formed a web, with them at the centre, just him and her. He found it hard to imagine suddenly being alone again.

Really?

Don't worry.

He watched her as she played with her cigarette. Don't worry, she'd said. He thought about that. Then he said: If you don't come back, I'm coming to get you.

I'll hold you to that.

She turned onto her side and put the cigarette down on the bed, with the lighter beside it.

When exactly are you going?

Two weeks' time.

I'll take you to the airport.

Are we walking?

We'll get a taxi.

Ragna thought about it. No, I'll take the train.

Then we'll take the train together. I want to see you off.

She nodded.

How long's the flight?

About ten hours.

They won't let you smoke, will they?

I was planning to give it up anyway, she said. She lit her cigarette, placed the lighter beside the saucer and blew a thin column of smoke towards the ceiling. He looked at her face. He kissed her neck, slid the sheet aside and kissed the small of her back. She pressed her face into the pillow. He stroked her back, her shoulders. Pressed his cheek against her shoulder blade. Her scent was stronger than the smell of the cigarette. He growled and Ragna made small sounds that were buried in the pillow. Then he pulled her pants down and she turned over.

What's wrong?

I don't know.

He lay beside her.

You're going to have problems on that plane if they don't let you smoke.

I told you, she said, I'm giving it up. Her hand with the cigarette hovered above the floor. Some ash fell, missing the saucer.

*

The road rises slowly and the horizon stretches away into the distance. They crawl towards the horizon, crest the hill and see a new horizon in front of them, even more distant than the previous one. As they drive down the other side, Danny asks: Are you going next year?

Robert looks over at him. Why do you ask?

Or won't she let you?

Robert thinks. I didn't even see that bull, he says.

Which bull?

The one that hit me. I didn't see one single bull. It's the first year I haven't seen a single bull.

So you want to go back next year to see another bull.

Maybe.

Danny moves his hand to the bottom of the steering wheel, wraps his thumb around it and says: It was brown.

Brown?

Yes. The bull was brown. That's all I remember.

Robert's thinking. He keeps fiddling with his leg. After a while, he says: What about you?

What?

What are you going to do when you get back?

First I'm going to take you home.

They get stuck behind a car towing a caravan. A line of other cars overtakes them. Danny waits silently for a gap. They look at the windows of the caravan, which are hung with nets. Danny follows it for a long time, long enough to study the stickers displayed above the bumper. A mountain landscape. A birdhouse that looks like a cuckoo clock. A beach with a Spanish name. When they've finally overtaken the caravan, Danny asks: Would you do it again?

Robert hesitates, then says: In a heartbeat.

The end of the toll road comes into view, followed by a two-lane stretch with a turn-off. A few kilometres later, a new toll road begins. Danny steers the car through one of the tollgates. Robert hands him some money. He pays, takes the ticket and heads for the filter that turns the road back into three lanes. There are cows on the other side of the crash barrier, red cows with their heads to the grass. It looks as if they're zooming past the car. He's thirsty but he doesn't want to disturb Robert, who has the bottle by his feet.

What about you? Would you do it again?

His foot is on the accelerator. He realizes that with every passing second, every metre he leaves behind, he's getting closer to her. And to him. He tries not to think about them.

Yes, he says.

Robert shakes his head. You wouldn't.

Danny thinks about his attic room. That's getting closer by the second too. And his bed. And the skylight. He looks over at Robert's leg and the plaster, at his pained expression, and he feels the car vibrate, feels the wheels turn, feels the engine drone. His head seems to be vibrating too. His arms hold the steering wheel tight, his whole body buzzing with vibrations. A powerful feeling tingles from his heart through his veins, a feeling that is right for him now, just as the sound of the engine is right for the car. It spreads through his body, through his limbs, to his head, where images loom, images of Ragna and the other man and of what Danny did to them. Amplified by those images, the feeling descends into his body, his heart, and spreads until it's not clear where it begins and where it ends, because it's completing circuits through his bloodstream. He clenches his jaw. New images appear in his head, so horrifying and at the same time more realistic than the previous images, like a nightmare.

A large red Renault overtakes them. He sees a girl of about four in the back. She's standing on the seat, her face pressed to the glass, which is steaming up. Colourful farmyard characters are stuck to the window. A horse, a cow, a farmer with something in his hands. A barn and a lot of red and yellow and green chickens. She waves at him. Danny manages to raise his hand. The girl waves even more enthusiastically and then disappears into the distance.

*

High above them, an aeroplane draws a white line in the sky. Danny moves closer to the windscreen. The aeroplane sets course for the west. He slowly leans back into his seat. The plane glides above them in a wide arc, over the windscreen, over the roof, until it vanishes behind his left shoulder. Danny slows down a little. The car edges towards the hard shoulder, almost as though it's steering itself.

The motorway's quiet. A lone car passes them, blows its horn.

Robert looks over at him. Hey, he says.

Danny grips the wheel, sits up straight, accelerates and sends the car shooting up the motorway again. He rejoins the traffic without looking in the rear-view mirror. The toy car in the glove compartment rolls back and forth. It bumps into the side and rolls back again. Then it's still.

*

He looked up at the endless line of monitors in the departure hall. The names of the cities and the numbers of the flights changed. He couldn't see Bangkok. Ragna had phoned him the day before with the departure time and said it'd be better if they took separate trains. She'd go via WTC and he could go straight from Centraal Station. He looked at the monitors again. There were only flights to Geneva and Boston at the time Ragna had given him. A family came over and stood beside Danny, a man and a woman with three daughters. The youngest was still in a pushchair. Their suitcases were stacked on a trolley.

What flight are you looking for?

Bangkok.

Bangkok?

Yes.

What time?

Half eleven.

Isn't it up yet?

Those are the twelve o'clock flights.

The man looked at the monitors. I can't see it either.

Thanks, said Danny. He walked to the departure hall and looked at the signs, trying to find an information desk. A woman in a uniform was standing in the middle of the hall.

She was talking to an Asian-looking man. When he'd gone, Danny went over and spoke to her.

Excuse me. What time does the Bangkok flight leave?

Which airline?

I don't know.

Aren't you a passenger?

I've come to see someone off.

The woman took out her PDA and pressed a few buttons. Bangkok, she said quietly. Then: There's only one flight to Bangkok today and it's leaving in forty minutes.

That soon?

Yes, at ten past ten.

Are you sure?

That's the only flight to Bangkok.

Damn it. Which check-in desk?

Fifteen. That way. You might just catch them.

Danny headed in the direction the woman had indicated. He was almost running. He read the numbers on the yellow signs, counted down. The signs above the desks showed the flight numbers and departure times. There it was: ten past ten.

He went over to the stewardess at the Bangkok check-in desk.

The flight to Bangkok, have all the passengers checked in already?

Are you here to check in, sir?

No, I'm here to see someone off.

Check-in started just after seven.

And?

I'll have a look.

The woman moved her mouse and checked the screen. There's just one passenger who hasn't gone through yet. An Englishman. Is that who you're looking for?

No.

Then I'm sorry, but I can't help you.

Thanks anyway.

You can see the aeroplanes from the observation deck, the woman said, pointing at the escalators.

He went back to the departure hall, headed up the escalator and followed the signs to the observation deck. Outside, he leant over the railing and looked at the planes. There were several out there, but he didn't know the flight number or the airline. He stood there for a while, watching the planes as they trundled to the runway. Then he went back inside.

He walked past a refreshment area and saw Gerard Varon sitting in his wheelchair at a low table outside a snack bar. He was wearing a suit with a pink tie and was talking to a man of his own age, who was also in a suit. There were three younger men and a woman with them. One of them was a black guy Danny knew by sight.

He walked past the table. Gerard spotted him. He looked at Danny for a moment before raising his hand. Danny, he said.

Danny stopped.

You missed her.

Danny didn't respond.

Shame, said Gerard.

He stared at the man in the wheelchair, tried to work out from his body language and his expression what was really going on, but it didn't help. He walked over to the table. Gerard took his hand, gave it a firm shake and, smiling broadly, introduced Danny to the others. One of my better boxers, he added.

He turned to Danny. Did you get stuck in the traffic?

I had the wrong time.

It changed. Didn't she call you?

No.

She said she was going to call. Because you wanted to be here. They changed the time of the flight and she only found out yesterday. She phoned to ask if we could give her a lift. I had to come out here anyway.

Danny stood beside the wheelchair, towering above Gerard. No one pulled a chair over for him and he didn't want to take one himself.

Shame, Gerard said again. He looked over at the man on the other side of the table. See that guy? He's a middleweight champion from Los Angeles. He's got a plane to catch too.

The American boxer nodded at Danny.

In my line of work, you spend half your time sitting in the office, Gerard said, and the other half at the airport.

Danny looked out at the planes behind the large windows. In the distance, he saw one taking off.

Gerard looked up at him and asked: How's the training going?

Good.

You on schedule?

Yes, he said. He knelt down, put his hand on the arm of the wheelchair and said: When's that Argentinean coming to Europe?

Ramos?

Yes.

In plenty of time for the fight, said Gerard.

*

The sun shines in the wing mirror and streams in through the rear window, its warm light pushing them northwards. The car follows its own shadow as it glides over the tarmac. Road signs flash past, showing the distance to Paris. He speeds up. The numbers on the signs are counting down. They fly past the places whose names he saw on the way to Pamplona.

Have I thanked you yet? Robert asks.

What for?

For driving me home.

Danny rubs at the steering wheel. Robert manoeuvres himself into a different position, puts a hand on Danny's shoulder and gives it a gentle squeeze.

Thank you.

His foot twitches on the accelerator, as though he can shake off the hand by pushing down on the pedal. The hand slides away. He feels its weight on his shoulder for a long time afterwards. He sees the images of Ragna and Varon and he squeezes his eyes shut and takes it. For the first time, he takes it, and for the first time, a thought comes to him that feels right for the direction they're travelling in.

He says: I'd do everything differently.

What would you do differently?

Everything, if I had the chance.

I don't follow you.

You asked if I'd do the same again and I said yes. But that's not true. I'd do everything differently.

Robert looks over at him, shifts his leg. Then he looks back at the tarmac.

Yeah, all of it. Danny sniffs. He slides his hands around to the bottom of the wheel and back up to the top.

*

Just concentrate on getting ready for the fight, Varon had said to him at the airport. She'll be back before you know it.

So he did. As well as the usual evenings, he trained three afternoons a week and one morning. He dedicated himself to his training, improved his condition, worked on his explosive power, did lots of running and exercises to keep his body supple.

He often thought about her, but she didn't get in touch.

In mid-May, summer suddenly arrived. Danny kept on training in the boxing school's stuffy gym. Through the open windows, he could hear sounds from the tables outside the bar across the road, chairs scraping, people talking. The clink of glasses on a tray. Two dogs barking at each other.

He reached his maximum training levels three weeks before the fight. At the end of one of the training days, he realized he couldn't take it any longer and phoned Gerard Varon's office. Varon asked if everything was okay.

Yeah, fine, he said.

Is there something you need?

He said no.

Gerard asked him a few more things about his training and about the fight in Germany. The line went quiet for a moment. Then Danny asked: Have you heard from Ragna?

She phoned once, Gerard replied. To say she'd got there okay. And another time to say everything was fine.

Danny was silent.

If she phones again, shall I get her to call you?

Yes.

Okay? I can't do much more than that for you, son.

It's fine.

I'll tell her then, said Gerard. Bye, Danny. He rang off.

But she didn't call. He thought it might be difficult to call from Thailand. He asked Richard if he'd ever been to Asia. Or if he knew what the connections were like there. The phone connections. But Rich had never been and neither had Ron. Rich said: My dad sometimes used to go to Japan and Taiwan. He always told us not to expect him to call. I tried once and I just got an operator on the line, going on and on. If I hadn't hung up, I'd still be sitting there now, listening to the silly cow.

*

The music fades. After a few commercials, there's a beep and a woman's voice reads the news in French. Danny looks at the radio, at the lights and the buttons. His hand's on the gearstick, ready to give the radio a thump. His eyes scan the dashboard and then slide back to the road. The Renault in front of them must be twenty years old. Danny changes gear, steers into the left-hand lane and lets the engine drown out the newsreader's voice.

*

Rich showed him a cardboard tube. He took off the lid and slid out a roll of posters. Take a look at these, mate.

Danny watched as he unrolled one of the posters. He was on the left, Ramos on the right. Above their heads were some words in English. He looked at the Argentinean. He had a square jaw, a scar on his cheek, dark eyes and blond hair. They both had naked torsos and were looking straight into the camera.

They just got here, said Rich. What do you think?

That hair has got to be dyed, said Danny.

Not necessarily.

Danny took another look. He snorted.

There are lots of Germans in Argentina, you know. They've got plenty of blond people over there.

Yeah, but that's dyed, said Danny.

Richard rolled up the poster and slid it back into the tube with the others.

I'm going to put a few of them up, he said.

The day of the fight was approaching. Danny could sense the tension growing, felt it in his stomach as he came into the boxing school. He'd shifted the emphasis of the training sessions to sparring and was planning a morning of intensive work. He warmed up with some skipping. The red rope was swishing in front of his eyes when Pavel came in. He shouted something from the corridor and disappeared into the changing room. A few minutes later, he came into the gym in his training gear. He turned on the interval bell and they started their programme. First a series of jabs, which Danny did at seventy-five per cent. Relax, relax, Pavel kept on saying. Keep your calm. He held the pads tightly and blocked Danny's jabs. After the bell, he said: I give that Ramos five rounds.

The bell rang again, for a new interval. He repeated a series of left, left, right hook, with the last jab an uppercut that Pavel blocked with his glove at chin level.

Pavel said: No time between the jabs.

Danny jabbed.

The bell went.

Good, said Pavel. Good work. Danny's black T-shirt was dripping with sweat. They took a break. He fetched his water bottle and passed it to Pavel.

Could you take the top off?

Pavel opened the bottle, handed it back, and Danny squirted water into his mouth. It dripped down his chin and onto the floor.

He's going to be a happy man.

Who?

Varon. This is seventy-five per cent. If you give it a hundred in Germany, maybe even a little more, he'll be delighted.

He knows what I can do.

That's true. I was talking to him about you just now, in one of those cafés round the corner.

Varon? You spoke to Varon?

Yes. He has a high opinion of you.

What did you say?

That you're doing well.

The bell rang loudly.

Now another series, said Pavel. Left, left, bend your knees, and a right hook straight on the body.

Holding the pads firmly, he stood opposite Danny, his left leg in front of his right. They worked through the series. No time between jabs, Pavel repeated again and again. Danny flashed his gloves in and out, pulling them cleanly back to his face.

After the bell, Danny asked: What else did he say?

What about?

About the fight.

He said that more than half of the tickets have already been sold.

Danny pressed a glove to his ear. Other than Pavel's breathing, there was no sound. No noise from outside, no people in the corridor or in the canteen. Danny thought about Ragna and about Gerard Varon. For a moment, he felt genuine pity for the man, who was grey and getting old.

He said: That's nice for him. His voice was softer.

Yeah, Pavel agreed.

They waited for the clock and, just before the bell rang, Pavel said: Yeah, life's treating the boss well.

What do you mean?

Told me he's going to be a daddy.

Danny looked at him.

Pavel said: He was eating cake with that girlfriend of his and he showed me the ultrasound. One of those printout things on shiny paper, you know. They'd just had it done.

Which girlfriend?

That Asian girl.

Danny stood there, stunned.

Pavel carried on talking, said it was quite an achievement for a man in his condition, if you thought about it. He said he was pleased for him and asked Danny if he'd already heard the news, because he wasn't saying anything. Then Pavel said something else, but the sound seemed to be absorbed by the walls.

Come on, said Pavel.

Danny just stood there.

Another round or do you want to do some stuff on the wall pads?

Pavel walked over to the black pad on the wall. When he turned around, Danny was taking off his second glove and throwing it into the box by the wall. He unwrapped the bandages, pulled the loops over his thumbs and dropped them on the floor.

Which café are they at? he asked.

*

It's night. The motorway up ahead is dark. Red rear lights hover at regular intervals in front of their car. They approach a petrol station with a shop.

Need a rest? asks Robert. Or do you want something to eat?

Danny nods, takes the exit and parks in one of the bays. The car park's deserted. Danny picks up the water bottle and drinks. He hands it to Robert. They leave the doors open. Danny puts his left foot on the ground, moves his other foot around to loosen up his leg muscles.

Tired?

Could be worse, says Danny.

What do you want to eat?

Just a sandwich or something.

Danny looks at the shop entrance and the harsh fluorescent light. There are no cars by the pumps, just an old lorry and three cars in the car park.

Could you go in and get it? Robert says, tapping his leg. Need some money?

Danny takes the banknote and gets out. He walks to the shop. The doors slide open. He goes inside and sees a rack of French newspapers with a few international newspapers on the bottom row. German, English. Two Dutch papers. He glances back at the car. Then he picks up one of the papers and looks at the date. It's today's. He reads the headline, runs his eyes down the news columns. There it is. He reads the report slowly, every word. The name of the café. The address. The man escaped with minor injuries. The twenty-four-year-old woman was taken to hospital. She was twelve weeks pregnant. It is unclear whether...

He puts the newspaper back on the rack, with the headline upside down. He walks over to the chiller cabinet, picks up the two nearest sandwiches, cheese rolls, walks to the till and gives the man the money. The man hands back some change.

Bon appétit, says the man.

Thanks, Danny replies.

Back at the car, he hands Robert one of the sandwiches and the change. They unwrap the rolls and eat them.

All he can think about is the newspaper report. He rests his hands on the steering wheel. It seems to vibrate slightly. He looks across the car park, at the lorry and cars standing still, the motionless trees sticking up into the sky around the edge of the car park, the bird of prey hovering in the sky above the trees. Everything has stopped. His thoughts slow to a standstill, become snarled up in the conversation with Pavel at the boxing school. He swears.

What's wrong? Robert asks.

Nothing.

Once the doors are shut, the isolation of the car is restored. Back on the motorway, only the droning of the engine breaks the silence. Danny puts his foot down.

Bring it on.

*

He walked around the outside of the boxing school, down a short road, before turning left onto a long, narrow street with a few spindly trees along it and scaffolding on some of the houses. He started walking faster. When he got to the square, he looked at the signs outside the cafés. Three men were standing around a couple of upturned wine barrels at the café on the corner. A van from a drinks company stood in the middle of the road and a fat man was pushing a trolley of crates through the door. On the other side of the square was another pavement café, with wicker chairs and tables and a few people outside. Café Kage was on its right. A row of chrome chairs stood outside, with small tables in front. Two women were sitting in the corner beside the windbreak, with a small dog between them. Danny skirted around a tree, got closer. Then he saw them, through the big pane of glass. Gerard Varon was in his wheelchair with his back towards him. He moved his hand in the air, clearly explaining something to her, and put it back on the armrest. Ragna was sitting beside him on the window seat, her back against the window, her hand in his lap. For a moment, he stood there and looked, as though he wanted to commit the scene to memory. On the table in front of them was a shot glass, a teacup, two forks and two plates, with crumbs on. He was aware of the smallest of details.

Then he'd seen enough. He stormed inside. The door flew open and he screamed something and it must have been a hurricane of sound, because everyone looked up and the music stopped, as if by some kind of agreement. He grabbed the arm of the wheelchair and swung it around. Gerard fell sideways against the table, slumped onto the floor, onto the yellow and orange tiles with the name of the café written on them. People screamed. He heard a woman shrieking. Not

Ragna. She slid back to the middle of the window seat and stared at him with huge eyes. He couldn't quite tell what emotion he could see in her eyes, fear, guilt or shame, but he knew that those dark eyes could not temper his fury, only increase it. He strode over to her. Gerard dragged himself across the tiles to the table, to the chair behind it, and tried to pull himself up. He groaned. Danny knelt down and thumped his cheekbone with his left fist. Gerard's head banged on the floor and he hid his face in his hands. Danny turned back to Ragna.

Danny, she said. Her voice was shaking.

He didn't react. He walked up to her and pulled her to her feet. He hissed something and pushed her into another table. She fell over and crawled away between two chairs, making for the shelter of the wall. A couple with a child had been sitting at the table, but they had fled to the back of the café. Danny hadn't noticed though. He only had eyes for her and for the wall and for the abandoned table she was hiding behind. He kicked it aside. The glasses fell onto the tiled floor and a teacup splintered into hundreds of tiny pieces. He grabbed her by the shoulders and hoisted her up against the wall. She wasn't looking at him now. She was holding one arm in front of her face, her other arm hugging her stomach.

On his way to the café, words had come flooding into his head. Words he wanted to say to her. You must think I'm stupid. Stupid fucking cow. You and that lame cripple. Did you really think it was going to work?

But now that he was standing there in front of her, he didn't say anything. His silence lasted a few seconds, but it felt like an eternity, because it was such a terrifying, threatening silence, as though every sound had ceased. As though a prophecy hung in the air.

Then he hit her. He hit her in the stomach, a hard left jab. Her head fell forward. He pushed her back against the wall and hit her, a right, then a left. It was like hitting a punch bag and having to hold it upright at the same time.

Ragna screamed. He hit.

A man from the café shouted something at him. Stop. Stop that! He put a hand on Danny's shoulder and pulled, but Danny elbowed him away and punched him on the side of the head. He went down.

He heard another shout, a different voice. Danny didn't react and no one dared to come closer. Danny hit again and nobody did anything. The only sound that got through to him was the sound of his fists on her stomach. People came over from the tables outside and stood looking in the window, crowding around to see. In a flash, between two series of jabs, he saw the fat man from the drinks company. His mouth was hanging open. Danny pushed her against the wall again. She made a quiet groaning sound. He swore. He looked at the window, saw a man with a mobile to his ear. He swore again, squeezed his eyes shut, clenched his jaw and hit for the last time. Then he stopped. He let her go. Ragna collapsed, slid onto the coloured tiles and lay crumpled on her side. No one said a word, everything was silent. Danny glanced down at her and turned to the door. He didn't even hurry. The people in the doorway stepped aside as though he'd asked them to. He stood there and took one last look around, saw her leg and her tangled hair, the bruise forming above her swollen eye. She clasped her hands over her stomach, lay there so still, her fingers limp and weak.

And he left.

He heard a siren in the distance. When he looked down the road, all he saw was the dark clouds approaching over the roofs of the houses.

*

They take two more short breaks during the night, to get something to drink and fill up with petrol. Otherwise they keep driving. Robert falls asleep. When the sun comes up, they're at the border between France and Belgium. About an hour later, they're getting close to home. Robert wakes up. He rubs his eyes and takes a swig of water from the bottle that Danny's just drunk from. Danny's following the motorway they took on the way down south. They pass the petrol station where he stood hitchhiking two days ago. It's dry now, but there's a veil of mist in the air. The motorway becomes busier and they end up in a traffic jam. They inch forward until Robert signals that they should take the next exit. Danny follows the signs to the village where Robert lives. Past that church tower, Robert says. Take a left. Robert taps his foot on the plastic mat beneath the dashboard. They go over a roundabout. Robert points at a side street. Danny drives down the street, over a couple of sleeping policemen.

Number twenty-seven, says Robert.

Danny looks at the house numbers on the left side of the street.

Behind that Land Rover.

Danny parks in the drive behind the Land Rover. He sees a tile with the number twenty-seven on the front of the semi-detached house. A path leads from the drive to the front door. There's a green fence around the garden. They sit together in the car for a moment, without saying a word. Then he hears a voice. A boy is running out of the front door. He's bigger than in the photo and his face looks older. He runs to Danny's side of the car, stops in his tracks, looks past Danny to his dad, and then dashes around to the passenger side. Robert opens the door, holds out his arms and gives the boy a hug.

Daddy, says the boy.

Robert's little girl comes out too, in less of a hurry. His wife appears behind her. She stays inside the doorway. The girl stops at the open car door. Hi, Dad, she says.

Danny sits there motionless at the steering wheel until the boy looks over at him and Robert says: This is Danny.

The boy nods. Danny holds out his hand. The boy shakes it.

My name's Eddie.

Hi, Eddie, says Danny, letting go of his hand.

And that's Sara and that's Manuela, Robert says.

Do you want me to help you? Danny asks Robert.

If you like.

Danny gets out, walks around the back of the car and helps Robert out. As Robert balances on one leg beside the car, holding on to the door, Danny turns around, opens the glove compartment, takes

MORGEN ZIJN WE IN PAMPLONA

out the Alfa 1300 and slips it into his pocket. He puts his arm around Robert's shoulders and they walk slowly to the front door. Manuela steps aside. They go into the house, down a hallway and into the living room.

Danny pulls back a chair and Robert sits down. The boy and girl have followed them. They look at Danny standing there, so big and wide in the small room.

Manuela walks over and stands on the other side of the table. Thanks, she says quietly.

Don't mention it.

Would you like something to drink? Robert asks. Something to eat?

No, thanks. There's no need.

Robert shows his plaster cast to his son. I'll let you draw something on it later, he says. He looks up at Manuela and says: I think I'd like a sandwich.

We're out of bread.

Danny goes over to the window. The girl's hiding behind Robert and staring out at Danny.

Danny's a boxer, says Robert.

A boxer? The little boy grins. I've got a boxing game for my computer.

Why don't you go and get it? says Robert.

The boy goes to the computer desk in the corner, looks through the shelf of games and comes back with one. The picture on the front shows two boxers. One's taking a swipe at the other, whacking him on the cheek.

He's the best one, says the boy, pointing at the blond boxer.

Do you want to be that one? asks Danny.

Yes.

Is his name Eddie too?

Yes.

Danny takes the blue Alfa out of his pocket.

Is this yours? Danny gives him the car. The boy looks at the toy car, turns it over and spins the wheels.

The door broke, says Danny.

That doesn't matter, does it? says Robert.

The boy looks at his father, then back at the toy car. He shakes his head.

I should go.

Do you want us to drop you off somewhere? asks Robert.

There's no need, says Danny. I can walk.

It's not far to the station, says Robert.

Danny takes a step towards him.

Thanks, says Robert.

No. I should be thanking you.

They shake hands.

Robert tentatively slides forward, takes a twenty-euro note from his pocket and holds it out to Danny.

For the train.

Thanks.

Take care.

I will.

Do you know what you're going to do now?

No, says Danny. He turns and walks to the door. He waves at the children, nods at Robert one last time and goes out into the hallway. When he reaches the front door, he hears Robert say: Let him out, will you?

It's a while before Manuela follows him. He's already opened the front door, but he stops on the doorstep. Manuela holds on to the edge of the door.

The station's that way, she says.

Thanks for bringing him back, she adds. Her voice is deep. Deeper than before.

He looks into her eyes and sees that their colour is warm, but her gaze is ice cold. Most of her body is hidden behind the heavy door.

Don't mention it.

Danny wants to ask her something, but she beats him to it.

It was in the paper, she says.

He nods.

Your photo was too.

She opens the door a little wider and Danny expects her to come outside, to say something else. But she stays there, half-hidden behind the front door, and doesn't say a word. She just looks at him.

I have to go.

Bye then, she says.

He nods. When he reaches the gate, he hears the door close.

He shuts the gate behind him and walks down the road, on his way to the station. He buys two waffles at the station kiosk and, with the change in his hand, he heads for the waiting room and sits down on a bench. The platform's empty. Before long, an elderly couple appear and soon other people are walking up and down the platform. He watches an express train go by. Then a commuter train stops. Some people get off. New passengers slide onto the vacated seats and the train slowly pulls out of the station. Through the dirty windows of the waiting room, he looks out at the platform and the nearby park and houses. His stomach rumbles. He tears open the plastic wrappers, eats the waffles and waits.

Out 2010
PEIRENE TITLE NO. 1
Beside the Sea by Véronique Olmi
translated from the French by Adriana Hunter

"A mesmerising portrait ... it should be read." THE GUARDIAN
....

PEIRENE TITLE NO. 2
Stone in a Landslide by Maria Barbal
translated from the Catalan by Laura McGloughlin and Paul Mitchell

"understated power" FINANCIAL TIMES
....

PEIRENE TITLE NO. 3
Portrait of the Mother as a Young Woman
by Friedrich Christian Delius
translated from the German by Jamie Bulloch

"This is a small masterpiece." TLS

Out 2011
PEIRENE TITLE NO. 4
Next World Novella by Matthias Politycki
translated from the German by Anthea Bell

*"A page-turning pleasure ... this novella has a supreme lightness
of touch ... It never feels weighed down by its own significance."*
ROSIE GOLDSMITH, BBC
....

PEIRENE TITLE NO. 5
Tomorrow Pamplona by Jan van Mersbergen
translated from the Dutch by Laura Watkinson

*"An intense reading experience ... Van Mersbergen tells what
needs to be told and not a word more."* DE MORGEN
....

PEIRENE TITLE NO. 6
Maybe This Time by Alois Hotschnig
translated from the Austrian German by Tess Lewis

"He is one of the best writers of his generation."
SÜDDEUTSCHE ZEITUNG

Peirene

Contemporary European Literature. Thought provoking, well designed, short.

"Two-hour books to be devoured in a single sitting: literary cinema for those fatigued by film." TLS

---

www.peirenepress.com

Peirene Press is building a community of passionate readers.
We love to hear your comments and ideas.
Please e-mail the publisher at: meike.ziervogel@peirenepress.com